MONTANA MAVERICKS

Welcome to Big Sky Country, home of the Montana Mavericks! Where free-spirited men and women discover love on the range.

LEGACY OF TENACITY

It's time to illuminate Tenacity! As the town begins to heal from its scars and scandals, its single cowboys (and cowgirls) are ready for a fresh start. They know that love can grow in the most unexpected places and that down doesn't mean out. So make a wish on a Montana moon for all to be revealed—they've waited for their sweethearts long enough!

A MAVERICK OF HONOR

Charity John is everyone's favorite. The cherished only daughter of a wealthy ranching family, she has always had things come easily to her...until now. From the moment she meets soldier Liam Martin, she knows he's The One. Liam says they're too different to make it work. He thinks he's protecting them both from heartbreak, but when he takes Charity in his arms, he is helpless against the tide of feelings that overwhelm him...

Dear Reader,

Have you ever met someone with whom you feel an immediate connection? It happens when Liam Martin sees Charity John at a military funeral, unaware that within twenty-four hours they will be formally introduced to each other. Although Liam is attracted to Charity, the former-military dog handler knows nothing will come of it. She is too young, and more importantly, they are from different worlds. As an heiress to a ranching dynasty, she is definitely out of his league.

Charity is struggling to assert her independence from her controlling parents, who insist she marry well. And for the Johns, marrying well means marrying someone who comes from wealth.

Liam is also facing a dilemma when it comes to Charity. Friends are telling him that if he is serious about her, then he's going to be in a fight because her parents will never approve of him, despite the fact that he's honorably served his country and has come home to his family's ranch as an injured veteran. With family drama high, Charity and Liam experience a roller-coaster of emotions threatening to derail any future they could have together.

I hope you will enjoy these two tortured souls whose love is strong enough for them to find healing.

Happy reading,

Rochelle Alers

A MAVERICK OF HONOR

ROCHELLE ALERS

MIX
Paper | Supporting responsible forestry
FSC® C021394

Special thanks and acknowledgment are given to Rochelle Alers for her contribution to the Montana Mavericks: Legacy of Tenacity miniseries.

PLEASE RECYCLE • THIS PRODUCT IS RECYCLABLE

Recycling programs for this product may not exist in your area.

ISBN-13: 978-1-335-54091-1

A Maverick of Honor

For questions and comments about the quality of this book, please contact us at CustomerService@Harlequin.com.

Harlequin Enterprises ULC
22 Adelaide St. West, 41st Floor
Toronto, Ontario M5H 4E3, Canada
www.Harlequin.com

HarperCollins Publishers
Macken House, 39/40 Mayor Street Upper,
Dublin 1, D01 C9W8, Ireland
www.HarperCollins.com

Printed in Lithuania

Since 1988, nationally bestselling author **Rochelle Alers** has written more than eighty books and short stories. She has earned numerous honors, including the Zora Neale Hurston Award, the Vivian Stephens Award for Excellence in Romance Writing and a Career Achievement Award from *RT Book Reviews*. She is a member of Zeta Phi Beta Sorority, Inc., Iota Theta Zeta Chapter. A full-time writer, she lives in a charming hamlet on Long Island. Rochelle can be contacted through her website, rochellealers.org.

Books by Rochelle Alers

Montana Mavericks: Legacy of Tenacity

A Maverick of Honor

Montana Mavericks: Behind Closed Doors

Lassoed by a Maverick

The Fortunes of Texas: Secrets of Fortune's Gold Ranch

To Catch a Fortune

Montana Mavericks: The Anniversary Gift

The Maverick's Thirty-Day Marriage

Harlequin Special Edition

Bainbridge House

A New Foundation
Christmas at the Château

Visit the Author Profile page at Harlequin.com for more titles.

Chapter One

Liam Martin closed his eyes as he listened to the solemn words of the army chaplain. The somberness of the military funeral weighed on him like a large stone on his chest whenever he stared at Dean Valentini's flag-draped coffin. He hadn't known Dean personally except that he had succumbed to his injuries months following the same explosion that had nearly ended Liam's life. It wasn't for the first time that he'd questioned why he had survived when Dean hadn't, and eventually realized he was experiencing survivor's remorse.

When he'd enlisted in the army after graduating high school, Liam had planned to become a lifer. However, his plan had been thwarted during an overseas combat exercise. He could still recall hearing the distinctive high-pitched sound of the bomb before it exploded, the plaintive howling of his dog, Harley, and the screams from the wounded before he'd been swallowed up by comforting blackness that had shut out everything around him. He'd been unconsciousness when he was airlifted to Landstuhl Regional Medical Center in Landstuhl, Germany, where he underwent a series of surgeries. The first time he'd been lucid Liam had asked about Harley and been told that it was Harley who'd pulled Dean to safety. Not only were military dogs large and powerful, but they were also very well-trained and disciplined. Harley, like all military dogs, had formed an unbreakable bond with his human partner, so separating him from Liam had probably not been easy for the German shepherd.

Even though the military did not allow handlers to keep their dogs, because Harley had apparently been experiencing PTSD from the explosion, permission had been granted for his dog to be shipped back to Liam's home in Tenacity, Montana. He'd arranged for Ryder Trent and his sister, dog groomer Renee, to care for Harley until he was discharged from the hospital, because he knew his parents were unable to take care of him.

Once he'd recovered enough from his more serious injuries, Liam had been transported to San Antonio Military Medical Center in the States for more surgery and rehab sessions. Now that he was finally stateside, Liam was anxious to return to Tenacity but had delayed his plans to make a stop in Bronco to attend the funeral of the fallen soldier.

When the chaplain concluded the service, he opened his eyes and stood up to leave, and that was when he saw a young woman sitting across the room, her blue eyes filled with tears; Liam wondered if she'd known Dean. He slowly blinked, thinking she just might be the most beautiful woman he had ever seen, then conscious of the seriousness of the occasion, he quickly dismissed the thought. She was a mourner, and he was on his way home to Tenacity.

Two days ago, the doctor at the VA hospital had approved his release, and now as a medically discharged veteran Liam would begin life anew as a civilian. Doctors and medics had told him over and over that he was lucky to be alive, and Liam felt doubly lucky that his canine partner, Harley, had also survived. He knew it was going to take time for him to adjust to being a civilian, but then all he had was time.

Liam hadn't told his family that he was coming home because he'd wanted it to be a surprise. And knowing his mother as well as he did, he was certain Maria Martin would have spent days preparing his favorite dishes, planning all the ways she'd fuss over him like a mother hen with chicks. As the youngest of Jack and Maria's sons, he'd always felt the need to assert himself and prove he was the equal of his two older brothers, Marco and Enzo.

He left the funeral service and walked to the rental car, unbuttoning the jacket to his dress uniform. Tenacity was nearly one hundred miles from Bronco, and the drive would give Liam enough time to prepare himself for a homecoming reunion with his family and Harley. A wry smile flitted over his mouth when he stared through the windshield behind the lenses of a pair of sunglasses. There had been a time when he couldn't wait to leave Tenacity, and now he couldn't wait to return. He'd done a lot of growing up and maturing in eight years and knew it would take time for him to stop thinking and reacting like a soldier. He was a son and a brother, and because his life had been spared, Liam wanted to make certain whatever he did in the future mattered. And that also meant working with his family to ensure the viability of the Double M.

Once he saw the signs indicating the number of miles to Tenacity, Liam experienced twin emotions of apprehension and excitement, hoping when reuniting with his mother she wouldn't become weepy. It was an emotion that he'd found more upsetting than anything. He'd recalled his mother crying when he'd told her he had enlisted, and then again, the first time he heard her voice once he was able to call her from the overseas hospital. Liam had attempted to reassure her that he was okay, when he actually wasn't, and then he was forced to hang up because Maria continued sobbing.

Liam bypassed Tenacity's downtown business district and took the local road that led to the Double M. He drove past a number of signs indicating family-owned ranches off in the distance. The largest ranch in Tenacity was still smaller than the smallest ones in Bronco—a town where those in Bronco Heights boasted thousands of acres and the ones in Bronco Valley were more modest; the difference was the ranches in Tenacity were barely scraping by year after year.

His family's Double M had survived because his father and brothers worked tirelessly to keep it sustainable, but things would change now that the family would have an extra ranch hand once Liam joined them. He knew it would take time for his body to heal completely, but that wouldn't stop him from assisting his father and brothers with their chores. He was also aware that his body would heal a lot faster than his mind. Not only was Harley showing signs of PTSD, so was his handler. Working the ranch, Liam hoped, would exhaust him and enable him to fall asleep and stay asleep without the disturbing images of the explosion and its aftermath that continued to plague him.

Liam wondered if his nightmares would ever go away. The army psychiatrist had reassured him that with time they would become less frequent yet couldn't promise they wouldn't reoccur without warning. The doctor had prescribed medication that would help to curb some of his anxiety, but Liam had refused it. He knew he had to be patient and hopefully there would come a time when the nightmares would completely vanish.

He drove past signs indicating the number of miles to the Coreys' Circle C and the Venturas' Split Valley Ranch, smiling. They were still operating. He hadn't been home in two years, yet he'd kept up as to what was going on in Tenacity when exchanging emails with family members. Now there was talk that Tenacity was experiencing a regeneration with the discovery of dinosaur bones. This truly was good news because after years of scandal that had impacted the town's financial viability, and had nearly led to its downfall, Liam believed Tenacity was more than entitled to a well-deserved resurgence.

He turned off onto the road leading to the Double M, slowing when he noticed new fencing along the boundary line. It had always been an ongoing task with repairing and replacing fences because ranchers were always at the mercy of the elements. Liam noted the time on the dash. It was late morning, and his mother was probably making lunch. Once she retired from teaching Maria had made it a practice to prepare breakfast, lunch and dinner for her family. It hadn't mattered that her husband and sons were able to cook for themselves, because she'd claimed cooking and teaching were her passions that kept her busy.

He maneuvered along a stretch of road that led to the rear of the large main house where he had grown up with his brothers. Once they'd reached adulthood they were able to move into their own cabins. It had become a running joke among his brothers that they'd moved away from home without actually leaving the ranch.

His mother's vehicle was the lone one parked in the back of the house. His father and brothers were apparently still working somewhere on the property. Liam gathered his rucksack from the second row of seats and made his way to the back door leading the mudroom. He slipped out of his shoes, leaving them on a mat with several pairs of boots, then walked quietly on sock-covered feet through the narrow hallway and into an expansive kitchen from which wafted mouthwatering aromas that reminded Liam he'd only had a cup of coffee earlier that morning. He'd checked out of the motel hours before dawn to make it to Montana by midday. He smiled, staring at his mother who was busy putting out place settings on the table.

"*Hola, bonita,*" Liam said softly in Spanish. He'd called his mother pretty, because she was. She been voted the prettiest girl in her high school graduating class, and even now in her mid-fifties she still turned the heads of most men whenever she entered a room.

Maria's hand halted setting down a knife as she stared at Liam as if he were an apparition. Her hand shook at the same time her eyes filled with tears. "Oh my," she whispered.

Liam chided himself for shocking his mother as she began crying. Taking long strides, he wrapped his arms around her petite body and dropped a kiss on the black hair with more streaks of gray than when he'd last saw her. Once his family was informed that he was going to be transported to a stateside hospital, Liam extracted a promise from his father that he would come alone, because he didn't want his mother to see him swaddled in bandages and connected to machines monitoring his vitals.

His brother Enzo had accompanied Jack, while Marco had remained behind in Tenacity with their mother. He had been sedated when they'd arrived, and the attending doctor had explained to his family that he'd undergone a second round of skin grafts on his face the day before and despite being heavily sedated, Liam managed to communicate to them that he was going to be okay with a thumbs-up gesture.

"It's okay, Mami. Don't cry," he whispered in her ear.

Maria sniffled as she buried her face against his chest. "I thought I was seeing a ghost. Why didn't you call to let me know you were coming home?"

Liam smiled. "I wanted to surprise you."

"What you did was nearly frighten me to death."

Easing back, Liam stared down at his mother's large dark tear-filled eyes. "Please don't mention death or dying. I've experienced enough of that over the past six months."

Maria nodded, patting his chest. "I'm sorry, *hijo*."

Liam had grown up bilingual; his mother and grandmother spoke Spanish and English to him and his brothers, while his dad had been slow to embrace to the language of his wife's ancestors.

Maria ran her fingertips over his face. "You are still handsome."

"That's because you're biased," Liam teased. Maria would brag to anyone who would stand still long enough to tell them that she had best-looking sons not only in Tenacity but in the entire state of Montana. His mother's Latino and his father's African-American genes had combined, and the result was a khaki-brown complexion that made him appear perpetually tanned, evenly balanced masculine features and dark brown curly hair, which Liam always wore cropped.

His mother smiled. "I'll admit to that." She sniffled again, then reached into the pocket of her bibbed apron, removed a tissue and blotted her cheeks. "Why don't you wash up while I finish making lunch. Your father and brothers should be walking through the door at any moment now." The words were barely off her tongue when Jack, Enzo and Marco Martin walked into the kitchen, all stopping short when they spied Liam.

Jack was the first to be galvanized into action when he

pulled Liam against his tall, lean body. "Welcome home, son," he said hoarsely, his deep voice trembling with emotion.

It wasn't often that Liam hadn't witnessed his father being other than the stoic man who was always in control of his emotions and everything around him.

Liam patted Jack's back. "Thanks, Dad. It's good to be home." Untangling himself from his father's embrace, Liam hugged Marco, then Enzo, who gripped Liam's chin and peered closely at his face.

"The plastic surgeons did a good job on your face. You won't scare off the ladies whenever they look at you," he said teasingly.

"Speak for yourself, Enzo," Liam countered, smiling. "You haven't had anything done to your face, and the ladies still don't look at you."

Marco burst into laughter at the same time he shook his head. "I guess he told you, big brother."

Enzo glared at Marco. "The only thing I'm going to say is that I get more action from the ladies than you do."

Maria shook her head. "Enough about who gets more action," she scoffed. "Three grown sons and I still don't have a grandchild!"

Jack gave Enzo a pointed stare. "See what you started," he said under his breath. "No more talk about women. Now, let's get washed up and eat."

The good-natured teasing, which was a holdover from their youth, ended with Jack defusing relentless ongoing snaps until Liam and his brothers couldn't come up with anymore. He knew it couldn't have been easy for his mother to deal with testosterone overload whenever her husband and sons all got together. Nor was it the first time that she'd mentioned wanting daughters-in-law and grandchildren whose photos she could show off to her retired friends.

For Liam, though, dating wasn't at the top of his list now that he was back in Tenacity. It wasn't going to be easy settling into life as a civilian, and he wanted to give himself time to ease into ranching.

What was easy was sitting at a table with his family and passing around the dishes his mother had lovingly prepared. Maria had made a shrimp-and-corn chowder, a chopped chicken salad with lemon-tarragon dressing and sliced peaches topped with whipped ricotta and toasted pistachio nuts.

Enzo touched a napkin to the corners of his mouth. "I saw that your vehicle has Texas plates. Did you drive up from Texas?" he asked Liam.

"Yes. I rented it in San Antonio, and plan to return it in Billings. It was nice driving through cities and towns that I've never seen before," Liam explained. What he didn't say was he needed to get his head together before coming home. He'd continued to tell himself that he was okay, when in reality he wasn't. Not with the recurring nightmares that kept him from a restful night's sleep.

"Whenever you're ready to turn in the rental, I'll go with you and bring you back," Marco volunteered.

"Thanks, bro. We can do that tomorrow afternoon." Liam always felt closer to Marco because they were only two years apart, while Enzo was four years his senior. He smiled at his mother. "Mami, everything was delicious, but I'm going to change and go pick up Harley." During his layover in Nebraska, he'd texted Ryder that he'd be picking up Harley today. He was anxious to reunite with his canine partner. It had been much too long since he'd seen

Harley, and he hoped their reunion would be as momentous as what he'd just experienced with his human family.

Maria smiled. "If I'd known you were coming, I would've aired out your cabin before you got here."

Pushing back his chair, Liam stood. "That's okay. I'll stay here tonight and move in tomorrow." He'd taken up residence in one of the cabins on the ranch the year he turned twenty-one; the only time he'd slept there was when he was home on leave two years ago.

Liam gathered his rucksack and made his way up the staircase and to the bedroom where he'd grown up. He lingered long enough to send Ryder a text, telling him he would pick up Harley within an hour, shower and change into jeans and a black T-shirt. The fading scars on his arms where he'd been hit by shrapnel were now barely visible. He discovered a pair of well-worn boots on a rack in the back of a closet and a Stetson on the top shelf. It had taken less than thirty minutes for him to exchange his military uniform for the attire of a rancher, and surprisingly it didn't feel strange. His parents had constantly reminded him that ranching was in the blood of both sides of their families and even if someone left the ranch, they would eventually return to their roots.

Grabbing his keys, he set off for Ryder's. It had been six months since he'd seen his dog, and Liam wondered about Harley's reaction to seeing him after their long separation. Several different scenarios went through his mind as he concentrated on the road. There was no doubt Harley would remember him, but would he resent not seeing him for such a long time?

As he pulled up, he saw Ryder waiting with Harley. Shutting off the engine, Liam got out and walked over to Ryder, his gaze focused on Harley. Man and dog regarded each other for nearly a full minute before Harley jumped on Liam, his front paws resting on his chest, and he let out a distinctive woof. Liam buried his face in the thick fur and hugged his canine partner.

"It's okay, boy. I know you missed me as much as I missed you." Harley woofed again. "I'm going to take you to your new home and introduce you to my family. It's going to take a while before you become familiar with everyone, but there's no doubt they are going to love you."

Liam eased Harley down to stand, then extended his hand to Ryder. "I can't thank you enough for looking after Harley when I was unable to take care of him."

Ryder smiled as he took the proffered hand. "Welcome home, and there's no need to thank me. Harley's a great dog, and me and my sister, Renee, loved taking care of him."

"If there anything you need or want me to do to return the favor, then just let me know," Liam said.

Ryder smiled, his blue eyes filled with merriment as he shook his head. "Forget it, Liam. We didn't volunteer because we wanted something in return. It took a while for Harley to get used to me, but after a while we became best buds."

Liam stared at the tall man with tousled dirty-blond hair and blue eyes who had been rumored to be a Tenacity Romeo and had dated practically every girl in town. "What about a gift for your wedding?"

Ryder's smile was replaced by a sheepish grin. "You've heard about that?"

It was Liam's turn to smile. "Come on now, Ryder. I may have been on the other side of the world for the past two years, but that doesn't mean I don't know about things that go on in Tenacity. Thanks to social media I'm aware that you and Ella McIntyre are planning to tie the knot."

Ryder lowered his eyes, staring at the toes of his boots. "You've got me there." His head popped up and he smiled. "She's incredible."

Liam was more familiar with Ella than Ryder because she was one grade behind him in school. She was a naturally pretty girl who shared Ryder's coloring. "I'm glad for you and Ella."

He nodded. "Thank you. What about you, Liam? I know you've been gone a long time, but do you have any plans to settle down in Tenacity now that you've retired from the army?"

Liam wanted to tell Ryder that he hadn't retired but had been given a medical discharge. He'd save that for another day. "I've come back to help my family run the Double M."

"It's funny how a lot of folks can't wait to leave, then when they come back it is to stay."

"That's because there's something about Tenacity that keeps pulling you back even if you don't want to," Liam told Ryder. "Our family's roots run deep here, and even if I did become a lifer I still would have come back to the ranch."

"Speaking of ranches, at some point when you feel up to it, we can go visit Renee at the Stargazer. She's been thinking about expanding her dog-grooming business. She claims she needs your expertise when it comes to dogs."

"Let her know I'll help her any way I can, but I need some time settling in." It was the least he could do to repay Renee for taking care of Harley.

"I understand, and I'm certain she'll appreciate that." Ryder pointed to a large box. "She packed up his food, bedding, leash, lead and grooming supplies. I'll carry it to your vehicle for you while you get Harley settled inside."

Liam opened a door behind the driver's seat, then tapped a button on the fob to open the hatch. He motioned with his hand, and Harley jumped up onto a rear seat. He waited for Ryder to set the box in the cargo area, then close it.

He shook Ryder's hand again. "Tell Renee I'll be in touch in a week or two."

Ryder nodded. "I'll definitely let her know."

Liam got into the SUV, smiling up at the rearview mirror when Harley settled down on the second-row seats. His homecoming was complete now.

He arrived at the Double M and introduced Harley to his mother, carefully watching for her reaction to the newest member of the Martin family, while the dog sat quietly surveying his new surroundings. Liam placed the dog bed in an alcove off the kitchen and commanded him to stay.

"He's very quiet," Maria remarked.

"That's because he's been trained not to bark."

"He's also very big."

Liam met his mother's eyes. "His size is a deterrent, and that's why police departments and the armed services use them. Navy SEALS and the Secret Service favor Belgian Malinois over German shepherds, though. They're smaller but just as effective in taking down a suspect."

"Aren't those the dogs the soldiers carry over their shoulders and take with them when they parachute out of planes?"

A chuckle rumbled in Liam's chest. Being married to a former soldier had obviously made his mother familiar with military maneuvers. "Yes."

Maria walked over to the fridge. "I know you just had lunch, but what do you want me to make you for dinner?" she asked, changing the topic of conversation.

It's about to begin. His mother was preparing to hover over him like a helicopter mom, and he knew he had to move into his cabin as soon as possible and then join his father and brothers working the ranch to prove to Maria that he wasn't helpless. He'd understood her concern for his well-being but fortunately he'd cheated death to return home to loved ones.

Word of Liam's return must have spread like wildfire. An hour later a steady stream of people came to the house, intent on treating him as if he were celebrity. He noticed his mother's distraught expression as the voices from the crowd of well-wishers escalated and triggered Harley's barking. Liam felt himself withdrawing, besieged by all of the attention as Harley's barking became more frenetic.

It wasn't just the exhaustion from the two-day drive from Texas to Montana. There was something about hearing so many voices at the same time that reminded him of the chaos that had followed the exploding bomb before all the noise and pain vanished once he'd lost consciousness. He needed to get away from it. Not only did he need to get away from it, but he wanted to get back to a normal life.

He excused himself and managed to get his mother's attention. "I'm going to my room to lie down for a while," he said into her ear. "Please call me when dinner is ready."

He didn't know if anyone thought he was being impolite by disappearing when they'd taken the time to come welcome him home, yet in that instance Liam knew he had to put some distance between himself and the noisy crowd in the family room.

Maria placed a hand on his arm. "I saw that you were getting upset, so I'm going to ask everyone to leave. Go and rest," she said quietly.

Liam motioned for Harley to follow him upstairs. Once he entered his bedroom, he flopped down onto the bed.

Harley jumped up on the bed and snuggled next to him. It only took minutes for both to fall asleep.

However, sleep wasn't as kind to Liam. The nightmare returned, and he could hear an explosion followed by screams and then moaning.

The dream ended, but instead of waking up shaking and sweating before he was swallowed into a black hole, it was the image of a young woman with blond hair and blue eyes who'd reached out to pull him to safety. His pounding heart slowed, and within minutes he was able to drift into a deep, dreamless sleep, temporarily keeping his demons at bay.

Chapter Two

Charity John's melodious voice filled the interior of the Range Rover, her vocals blending with those of Andrea Bocelli and Sarah Brightman, singing "Time to Say Goodbye." She'd spent the one-hundred-mile drive from Bronco to Tenacity engaging in a one-woman concert as she sang along with her favorite songs.

Singing had become an extension of who she'd become, and Charity had to credit her sister-in-law, Marisa, for helping her gain the confidence to do things with her voice she hadn't thought possible. Marisa Sanchez-John, Tenacity's musical director, had been selected to coordinate Bronco's Mistletoe Pageant two years ago, and it was not only a rousing success, but Charity was able to gain the sister she'd always wanted when her brother Dawson had fallen in love and wed Marisa. Not that Charity's parents were overjoyed with the woman their son had chosen. In fact, Mimi and Randall John felt all three of their sons could've picked someone more suitable. "Suitable" meaning a ranching heiress who was either a Taylor or Abernathy, two of the richest ranching families in Montana. It wasn't that the Johns weren't wealthy, but they were just not as affluent as the other two.

As newlyweds, Dawson and Marisa had spent their

time shuttling between his hometown of Bronco and hers of Tenacity, and that was when Charity got to see them. Then Dawson decided to purchase a ranch in Tenacity, and while awaiting some construction projects to finish, he and Marisa had decided to stay in Tenacity and live with the Sanchez family until they could move to their own ranch.

Tapping a button on the steering wheel, Charity lowered the volume on the satellite radio the closer she came to Tenacity. Not only was she anxious to reunite with Dawson and Marisa, but she was looking forward to the town's long-awaited dinosaur dig restarting. Ever since a few dinosaurs bones had been found in Tenacity last year, there'd been a flurry of excitement...all of which was followed by controversy when the Bruckner family arrived in town claiming to own the land where the dig was to take place.

Though the initial dig had been planned to begin the month before, it was only now recommencing, after Tenacity's lawyers and the ones for the Bruckners decided to compromise. The Bruckners agreed to let the dig begin, with the understanding they would be able to share in the profits. It was now June and Charity was looking forward to joining the spectators. She was aware that the dig would go slowly, much like archeologists uncovering relics found in ancient burial sites, with hand tools like trowels and brushes. The delay and the legal controversy had only served to increase interest, both with the locals and in neighboring towns.

As she entered Tenacity's town limits, Charity noticed a number of people standing around in small groups. Hopefully she'd arrived before the dig was scheduled to begin. Slowing to ten miles an hour, she drove along a street behind a row of stores to find a place to park. She found one and pulled into an empty space between two pickups, got out and followed the posted signs that lead to the dig.

As she followed a crowd of spectators, Charity thought about Luca, Marisa's brother, whom she said was stoked because he was partially responsible for the Dinosaur Center becoming a reality. Charity laughed whenever Marisa teased her brother, calling him Dino-Man.

She found her sister-in-law among those who had gathered, hugging her as if they hadn't seen each other for years when it'd just been a couple of months.

Easing back, she smiled at Marisa. "Marriage definitely agrees with you."

A hint of color suffused Marisa's face. "You say that every time we get together."

"I say it because it's true." Her brother had taken one look at Marisa's long straight glossy black hair, large brown eyes and petite curvy figure, and as the saying went, *it was all she wrote*. "By the way, where's Dawson?" she asked, rising on tiptoe to scan the crowd for her brother.

"He got a call earlier this morning from the construction manager to come and look at the work on the main house. He just sent me a text before you got here that he's on his way."

"Do you have any idea when you'll be able to move in?" she asked Marisa.

"We're keeping our fingers crossed that it will be around the beginning of July."

"That's only four weeks from now."

Marisa nodded. "You're right. What I'm really excited about is decorating the rooms. You know you'll have your own bedroom suite whenever you come to visit us."

"You may come to regret saying that once I decide to move in permanently," Charity teased. For this visit she'd planned to stay a couple weeks.

"It would be nice if Tenacity could claim another John," said a familiar deep voice.

Charity turned and smiled at Dawson. He'd come up so quietly behind her that she didn't have time to react when he effortlessly lifted her off her feet while planting a loud kiss on her forehead.

"You look good, brother."

Dawson lowered her to stand. "That's because married life has been good. I recommend you try it."

A slight frown appeared between Charity's eyes. "Marriage isn't even on my radar." She wasn't anti-marriage, but at twenty-four she wasn't looking to settle down for at least another five or six years. She'd told herself that she had a lot more living to do, and that included traveling.

"What about dating?" Dawson questioned.

"That, too. Every once in a while, Mom drops a name of some boy from what she claims is a very good family she wants me to meet."

"Should I assume 'very good' means a well-to-do family?"

Charity gave her brother a side-eye glance. "You know exactly what she's talking about. Isn't that what she wanted for you, Jameson and Maddox—that her sons should marry heiresses?"

Grinning, exhibiting a set of perfect white teeth, Dawson nodded. "And that's what we didn't do. We married the women we'd fallen in love with, and we're living happily ever after."

Charity also smiled. "I do think Mom is softening up a bit. After all, she gave Marisa that platinum-and-ruby heart necklace that symbolized she'd accepted her as her daughter-in-law."

"I think it's because she became a grandmother," Dawson countered, referring to their brother Maddox and his wife Adeline's child, Matthew. "All of her sons are married, so that just leaves you, baby sis. And because Mom has never been the mother of the bride, she's going to put a lot of pressure on you to have a society wedding at the Association so she can show off for the Taylors and Abernathys."

"Not," Charity drawled, frowning. "I will not become a part of a spectacle just to please our mother." The Association was a private, members-only country club for wealthy Bronco Heights ranchers. It was by invitation-only, and Randall and Mimi John counted themselves among the privileged few who belonged. Charity didn't know why her parents, her mother in particular, continued to compete with wealthy ranching families when they were moneyed and considered old guard with deep roots in Bronco.

"Did we arrive too late?"

Charity shifted and smiled at Luca Sanchez. He'd put his arm around the waist of wife, Winter. "No," she said to Marisa's brother. "We're still waiting for the paleontologists to arrive."

"I overslept, so we had to rush to get here," Winter admitted.

Charity moved closer to Winter. "How are you enjoying motherhood?" she teased.

Winter ran her free hand over her brown hair she'd styled in a single braid falling midway her back. "I'm loving it. Marisa told me you're going to stay with us while you're here in Tenacity, so when we get back to the house, I want to show how I redecorated the nursery," she said without taking a breath.

Charity wanted to tell Winter that the house was not only going to be filled with Sanchezes but also Johns. Despite being one hundred miles apart, Bronco and Tenacity were becoming sister towns with the influx of Taylors, Hawkinses, Abernathys and now Johns settling in the latter. She'd grown up in Bronco Heights with upscale shops and boutiques, but she also felt equally comfortable browsing and shopping in Tenacity's small mom-and-pop businesses.

People continued to crowd into the area surrounding the dig as the paleontologists arrived and began working where a number stakes with colored pennants poked up from the earth. Charity glanced away for a second, then went completely still when her eyes met those of a man with a dog watching the dig. She closed her eyes in an attempt to remember when and where she'd seen him. Then it all came rushing back. The day before he'd come to Dean Valentini's funeral.

"Do you know who that man with the dog is, staring at us?" she whispered to Marisa.

Marisa turned her head to see who she was talking about. "That's Liam Martin. He's spent a lot of time in the military, but I heard yesterday that he's now back for good."

"How well do you know him?" Charity asked. She was curious as to why he'd attended Dean's funeral.

"He's an old friend of our family. Tenacity isn't that big, so everyone knows everyone. Do you want me to introduce you to him?"

"Please don't," Charity said, as she suddenly was overcome with shyness. "That's not necessary," she countered quickly.

Her protestations were ignored as Marisa waved to beckon him over. The man Marisa had identified as Liam Martin continued to stare at her, as if he'd seen a ghost. Well, she wasn't a ghost, but someone with whom he'd locked eyes for a few seconds twenty-four hours ago. And that had been enough time for her not to forget his face.

She hadn't realized how fast her heart was beating as she watched Liam and his dog coming in their direction. Seeing him up close caused her mouth to go dry when she stared at a pair of large dark brown eyes in a deeply tanned face with perfectly symmetrical masculine features under a black Stetson. There was something about the way he was staring at her that made it difficult for her to look away. Charity slowly blinked as she focused on the black T-shirt stretched across his broad chest that accentuated powerful biceps. She took a quick glance at the tattoo of a large dog on his left forearm. Liam Martin just wasn't just good-looking. He was gorgeous. Charity lowered her eyes and stared at the German shepherd standing motionless at Liam's side. She wanted to pet the dog but then noticed *K-9* and military stripes stamped on his harness and lead. It was obvious the shepherd was a military dog. She hadn't noticed the dog tags suspended on a chain around Liam's strong neck the day before because he'd worn his uniform.

"Liam, I'd like for you to meet my sister-in-law, Charity John. Charity, Liam Martin," Marisa said as she made the introductions. "Charity's going to be staying with my family for the next few weeks."

Liam extended his hand as a hint of a smile tilted the corners of his mouth. Charity also smiled when she took the proffered hand; it closed protectively over her much smaller one. The handshake was different from any other she'd shared with a man. There was something in its warmth that appeared to say, *You can trust me. I will take good care of you.* She knew she must have been hallucinating, or it was wishful thinking and she realized she was being ridiculous. She knew nothing about the man other than his name and that he was in the military, yet she felt an emotion that was totally foreign to her. Liam let go of her hand, and she immediately felt a loss of the connection.

"I'm sorry for not coming to see you when I heard you'd come home. But my family was so glad that you'd returned safely," Marisa said to Liam.

"It's okay," he replied. "I just got in yesterday, and once the word was out that I was back there was a steady stream of folks coming out to the ranch."

Charity met Liam's intense dark eyes. "Had something happened to you?" she asked.

"Not really," he said. "It would've been a lot worse if not for Harley pulling me to safety." He paused. "I saw you at Dean Valentini's funeral yesterday. How well did you know him?"

Charity motioned for Liam to move out of earshot from Marisa, because she didn't want her to overhear what she was going to tell him. She was never one to advertise who she'd been dating.

"I'd dated Dean briefly, but it was never anything serious. We hadn't spoken to each other in years, but when I heard what had happened to him, I wanted to pay my respects to his family. What was your connection to Dean?"

"I didn't know Dean personally even though we were in the same unit. I'd heard about his funeral, and because I was on my way back to Montana I decided to stop and pay my respects."

Her blue eyes grew wide. If Dean and Liam were in the same unit, then they must have been in the same explosion. "Oh, sweet heaven!" she whispered. "You could've died, too. I was told that a dog had pulled Dean to safety but unfortunately his injuries were so severe that he'd succumbed to them months later." Charity saw Liam staring at her, his eyes suddenly cold and hard as stone, and realized he was clearly uncomfortable with her talking about the incident.

"I'm so sorry, Liam, for bringing it up. It has to be painful for you to relive what you had to go through."

"It's okay," he said in quiet voice. "I'd rather look forward rather than backward."

She nodded and forced a smile. "You're right."

A beat passed before Liam said, "Maybe you can help me to look forward."

Charity gave him a puzzled look, wondering what in the world he was talking about. "How can I do that?" she asked.

"Go out with me."

Liam bit back a smile when he heard Charity's intake of breath. He knew he'd not only shocked her but had also taken her slightly off-guard with the request. And once the request was out, he knew it was impossible to retract it. He would later ask himself why, but right now he only knew he wanted to see Charity John again. And not during a solemn event.

"Okay," Charity agreed after what seem an interminable pause.

Smiling, Liam lowered his eyes. "Okay…or yes?" he asked softly.

"It's a yes, Liam. I'll go out with you."

Reaching into a pocket of his jeans, Liam took out his cell phone and handed it to her. "Please put your number in my Contacts, and I'll let you know when I can set up a place and time when we can get together."

Charity tapped her number into his phone, then reached into her crossbody to give him her phone. "You do the same."

Liam dropped Harley's leash. "Stay," he commanded in

a tone that the dog understood. He entered his phone number in Charity's cell and returned it to her. "Thank you."

Charity's pale eyebrows lifted questioningly. "For what?"

His gaze lingered on the blond hair she'd styled in a ponytail, then moved down to her brilliant blue eyes framed by long dark lashes before they came to rest on her petite nose and lushly curved lips. Charity John wasn't just beautiful. She was exquisite.

"For agreeing to go out with me." He paused as he saw Charity's hand tremble slightly as it covered her mouth. "Did I say something wrong?" Liam questioned.

She shook her head as an attractive flush darkened her fair complexion. "No, Liam. You're the first man in twenty-four years who has ever thanked me for agreeing to go out with him even before we have our first date."

Liam wanted to tell her that perhaps she'd been dating the wrong men. That with their inflated egos they might have just assumed because they'd asked, she would agree.

"If I take you to the Tenacity Social Club, will you have a problem being carded?" he teased, smiling.

Throwing back her head, Charity laughed, the sound reminding Liam of a tinkling bell. "No! I told you I'm twenty-four."

"Well, I had to ask because you look a lot younger."

"How young, Liam?"

"Someone who's not old enough to be served alcohol."

"And how old are you, Liam?"

"Twenty-six."

"Duh! You're practically an old man, huh?" she said, teasingly.

It was Liam's turn to laugh loud enough to draw the attention of those close enough to hear the outburst. In that instant he realized he hadn't been able to do that for six months.

"Older than you," he countered. Liam was hard-pressed to keep a straight face. Even before going out with Charity, he knew she would be good for him. The toothy white smile that lit up her entire face was infectious.

Charity pointed to Harley. "Will your furry companion join us?"

"No. Harley will stay home."

"Isn't he a service dog?"

Liam shook his head. "No. He's ex-military."

"How old is Harley?"

"Three."

"Ahh. He's still a puppy."

Liam wanted to tell Charity that Harley was hardly a puppy. He had been trained to search out explosives and narcotics and on command would attack and bring down a person and hold them captive until hearing a command to let him go. A roar when up from the assembly when the sliver of what was said to be a bone was uncovered.

"It's nice meeting you and I'm looking forward to our upcoming date," Charity said, giving Liam a warm smile before turning to walk away.

He watched Charity's retreat as she rejoined the Sanchezes, admiring the sensual sway of her slim hips in a pair of jeans that left nothing to his imagination. "I like her, Harley," Liam whispered under his breath. His dog looked up at him as if he understood what Liam was saying. "And I can't wait to see her again."

Liam hadn't planned to come to the dig, but when his mother told him about it over breakfast he'd decided to come and see what all of the excitement was about, and he was glad he did come because being introduced to Charity John was a pleasant encounter.

He and Harley walked to where he'd parked his vehicle and drove back to the Double M, stopping and parking the rental at the rear of his cabin.

Now he was former military and the owner of an ex-military dog who was his constant companion. He was also a Martin who was expected to join his father and brothers working the ranch that had been in the family for several generations. However, he knew it would take a while for him to become accustomed to life as a civilian, and knew he had to take it one day at a time.

Liam opened the rear door, wiped his feet on a mat, then left his boots on a stand in the mudroom as Harley wiped his paws on a mat. He patted the dog's head. "Good boy." He'd taught Harley to wipe his paws whenever he came in from outdoors.

Reaching for his cell phone, he sent Marco a text that he was ready to leave for Billings to return the rental. Less than ten seconds later he got a text from his brother telling him he would meet him at Liam's cabin around noon. Liam sent him a thumbs-up emoji. That would give him enough time to put up a load of wash and heat up some leftovers his mother had given him earlier that morning. The first thing on his agenda after returning the rental was a stop at Tenacity Grocery to stock his pantry and fridge. Maria Martin had taught all of her sons to cook, and Liam had come to enjoy spending time in his kitchen attempting to duplicate some of the delicious dishes that had been passed down to Maria from her mother, grand- and great-grandmother.

As he washed his hands in a half bathroom off the kitchen, Liam thought about possibly inviting Charity to the ranch for a home-cooked meal, then realized he was getting ahead of himself. They hadn't had their first date, and already he was thinking about her coming to his home—a place where he'd never invited another woman. He'd been gifted the cabin the year he'd celebrated his twenty-first birthday, but he'd spent less time sleeping under its roof than he had at the barracks and various bases stateside and overseas.

He wondered what was it about Charity John that had him thinking about her when he'd only caught a glimpse of her the day before and their interaction with each other earlier that morning hadn't lasted more than ten minutes. Her natural beauty and youthful appearance notwithstanding, it had been her dulcet voice and bright smile had drawn him to her. Interacting with her seemed to calm the demons that had continued to plague Liam when he least expected. And he still couldn't believe he'd asked her out when he wasn't interest in a romance or becoming *that* involved with a woman. His thoughts were running through his head like a runaway train as he wondered if going out with Charity was what he needed to pull him toward the light, even if it risked pulling her into his darkness. He said a silent prayer that it would be the former.

Drying his hands in a towel, Liam entered the kitchen and opened the refrigerator to take out one of the half dozen containers his mother had packed up for him. When he'd protested that she had given him too much food, Maria Martin gave him a look that he'd immediately recognized without her having to say it. *¡Basta!* There was to be no further discussion.

When he opened the container Liam realized there was enough chili for two persons. Maria had earned the reputation of making some of the best chili on the county, if not the entire state. Loaded with beans, meat, and topped with chopped raw onions and shredded cheddar cheese, it was non-stop eating. He spooned a portion into a microwavable dish to heat, while he refilled Harley's bowl with fresh water, his head going through mental calisthenics as to what he would prepare for Charity if and only if she felt comfortable enough to come to his home for a date night.

Chapter Three

Liam walked out of the car rental office in Billings and over to where Marco was parked. He opened the pickup's passenger-side door and got in. "Thanks, bro," he said, putting on his seat belt.

Marco smiled. "Anytime, little bro."

Liam shook his head. "When am I going to stop being your little bro?" he asked as Marco backed out of the driveway to begin the return trip to Tenacity.

"Never, because I'll always be two years older than you, and when we were young it was always my responsibility to look out for you. I can remember Mami saying, 'You have to make certain your little brother doesn't get into trouble bringing critters into the house that belong outdoors.'"

"That's because she lost it when I brought home that injured fox kit and told her we had to take care of it."

"Our mother took care of it all right when she called the wildlife sanctuary, screaming hysterically that they had to come to the ranch and get it out of her house. Then she waited outside until they finally took it away."

"It was only a baby, Marco."

"A baby fox that would grow into an adult predator."

Liam shrugged. "That was when I was in my wannabe veterinarian phase," he explained.

"You still haven't given up your love of animals. You became a military-dog handler."

"What can I say, Marco? I happen to like animals."

Marco gave Liam a quick sidelong glance. "What about women?"

"What about them?" Liam asked, answering his brother's query with a question.

"It's odd that I've never heard you talk about a girlfriend or about you dating someone special whenever you'd come home on leave."

Liam stared out the side window. "That's because there's never been anyone special. Being in the military and moving from base to base isn't conducive to forming lasting relationships. It was different with Dad because he and Mami dated in high school and throughout college, while I hadn't had a special girl in high school because I was focused on my coursework and playing baseball and landing a spot on the wrestling team."

"You did have a full plate." The seconds ticked, then Marco said, "You know, when we heard that you'd been in an explosion Mami was so upset we'd talked about having her sedated, while Dad walked around like a zombie for weeks refusing to talk to anyone about what had happened to you. Once you were shipped stateside, that's when everyone was able to exhale, knowing you were going to survive."

Liam had survived along dozens of others caught in the blast, while Dean Valentini hadn't. He didn't want to acknowledge that because Dean's military funeral had been held in Bronco, Montana, it had unknowingly connected him with a woman who'd once dated the deceased soldier.

He closed his eyes for several seconds. "There has to be a reason why I did survive."

Shifting into a higher gear, Marco increased his speed. “Have you figured out what that reason is?” he asked Liam.

“Not yet,” Liam answered truthfully. He knew he had to join his father and brothers working on the ranch, because that was a given. What he had yet to figure out was if there was another purpose for him to fulfill as gratitude for his survival.

“You’ve had more than eight years of military service and you’ve earned a degree in criminal justice. Have you thought about perhaps going into law enforcement?”

“If I did it would be as a K-9 trainer or handler.”

“I know it’s going to take time for you to get used to being a civilian, but whenever you’re ready for a little R and R we can go into town together and hang out at the Grizzly Bar or the Social Club.”

Liam didn’t want to tell Marco that he’d been thinking about taking Charity to the Tenacity Social Club. He had no intention of telling anyone in his family about Charity, and especially not before they had their first date. “Are you certain I won’t be a third wheel?” he asked Marco.

Marco chuckled. “If you’re hinting if I’m seeing someone special, then the answer is no. I have no intention of turning in my bachelor card for another few years.”

“Are you what folks call a serial dater?”

“No!” Marco protested. “That’s like the kiss of death in Tenacity. If word got out that I was seen with a different woman every other month, then I definitely would become persona non grata.”

“Tenacity’s fathers have always been protective of their daughters,” Liam stated, smiling.

“Word,” Marco drawled. “I took one girl out unaware that her father had put a tracking device underneath my vehicle.”

"How did you find out that it was there?"

"Dad discovered it. Most folks don't know that our father was a military electronic-intelligence technician and is currently a security consultant for a tech company. That's something he tries not to advertise. When Dad approached the man and handed him the device, I thought he was going to have a heart attack because it's a crime here in Montana to track a vehicle without consent."

"Did you ever take her out again?" Liam asked Marco.

"Hell no! I'm not going to deal with any woman whose family doesn't trust me to be with her."

"Same here," Liam said under his breath. He'd never taken advantage of any woman and hoped if their relationship was serious enough to contemplate planning a future together, he wouldn't have to deal with potentially hostile in-laws, and engaging in conflicts was something he intended to avoid wherever possible.

Settling back in his seat, he stretched out his legs while listening to Marco bring him up to date as to what was happening on the ranch. Jack Martin had purchased a bull when the old one had passed away, and he'd earned back the money he'd paid for him when Samson impregnated a number of heifers. The result was eight new calves.

"Enzo adopted a border collie a couple of months ago, and now with Harley the ranch has four dogs."

"I'm going to wait a few days before I introduce Harley to the other dogs on the ranch."

"Do you think they'll get along?"

"I'm certain they will once they acknowledge Harley as the alpha dog."

"Is there anything you need before we get back the ranch?" Marco asked when the sign indicating the number of miles to Tenacity came into view.

“If you’re not in a hurry to get back, I’d appreciate it if you stop at Tenacity Grocery so I can stock my pantry and fridge.”

Marco’s eyebrows lifted. “I know you like to cook for yourself. However, I’m going to suggest you come to the main house during your first week back so Mami can stop asking everyone if you are okay.”

His mother questioning if he was okay was the same question Liam had asked and continued to ask himself. There were occasions when he’d told himself yes, and then there were times when he had to acknowledge that he wasn’t okay whenever he’d experienced the recurring dreams about the explosion. Then there were times when he’d experienced panic attacks and he was forced to take deep breaths to calm himself. What he hadn’t identified were the triggers that precipitated the attacks.

“You have to know that our mother is a helicopter mom, Marco.”

“I know, Liam. Just try and humor her for a while so she can stop crying.”

“Crying?”

“Yes, bro. Our mother has tried to hold it together ever since you got back, but there are times when she’ll stop whatever she’s been doing and the tears just start flowing. The onetime Dad attempted to console her she screamed at him to leave her alone.”

Liam suddenly experienced twin emotions of guilt and selfishness as he’d tried to imagine what his mother had had to go through the last six months. The last eight years, in fact, when he’d been stationed around the world and out of touch.

“Now that you’ve told me that, I promise to share meals

with her. I know it's probably going to take her a while before she stops fretting over me."

Marco grunted. "Surely you jest. Maria Martin will continue to fret over her sons even after they're married and have families of their own."

"And then she'll become the doting *abuela*."

Marco laughed. "Now that you'll be eating in the main house, do you still need me to take you to Tenacity Grocery?"

"Yes," Liam replied, "I still need to buy some perishables and a few other staples."

"Copy that, Sergeant Martin. Is there anything else you'll need me to do for you?" Marco teased, grinning from ear to ear.

"Yes, there is. I need you to drive me to the garage so I can get a vehicle to use now that I'm back."

"Were you one of those badass sergeants barking orders and expecting privates and corporals to jump at your command?"

Liam laughed, the sound reverberating throughout the interior of the pickup. "No. I didn't have to bark. I had Harley for that."

It had taken only three days for Liam to feel as if he'd finally come home. He'd deliberately kept busy because it kept him from thinking about Charity. However, he knew he had to call her about their date or she would think he wasn't interested. He'd stocked his pantry and fridge with everything he needed, gotten up at dawn to drive to the main house to share breakfast with his family, then headed out to the stable to groom the horses, turn them out to graze while he mucked out and hosed down the stalls. Harley had accompanied him, and he'd watched intently while the other herding dogs approached the shepherd, heads lowered when they seemed to acknowledge him as their pack leader.

Once he returned home after eating dinner with his family, the topics of discussion included the increased price of feed for the ranch's livestock and machinations behind the mayoral election with JenniLynn Garrett winning the seat. Enzo talked about several Hawkins Sisters from the famed rodeo family who'd settled in Tenacity, and it was obvious several families from Bronco Heights had become so enamored with residents of Tenacity that not only had they married them but also decided to relocate.

Liam suddenly became alert when his mother mentioned Marisa Sanchez marrying Dawson John, and then he recalled Marisa introducing Charity as her sister-in-law. It was apparent Charity's brother had decided to live in Tenacity where his wife's family had lived for generations.

He was grateful when dinner ended because doing chores reminded him that his body hadn't totally healed. Sore back muscles and straining tendons in his neck, back, legs and arms were no doubt the result of his overdoing it. He'd established a ritual of returning to his cabin after dinner to sit on the porch and watch nightfall descend on the landscape as if someone had slowly pulled down a shade to conceal the waning daylight. Harley lay in a corner, his muzzle resting on front paws. His canine partner had taken to ranch life as if it was something he'd been born into.

Reaching for the cell phone resting on the cushioned rocker, Liam picked it up and scrolled through the contacts for Charity's number. He'd asked her to go out with him and she'd agreed, so now it was time to make that a reality. Liam sent her text asking if she would be willing to meet him at the Tenacity Social Club the following evening around seven. He didn't have long to wait for an answer when she sent him a smiley face and thumbs-up emojis.

Smiling, Liam set the phone on the cushion. "Well, partner," he whispered, "it's about to begin." Harley lifted his head when hearing his handler's voice, got up and ambled over to the side of the rocker to lie down again.

He ran his fingertips over the top of the dog's head, down his back, feeling solid muscle under the thick fur. He'd made it a practice to brush Harley every other day to keep his fur from matting. Renee Trent had recently groomed Harley, which had led to a lot less shedding.

Liam lost track of time as night blanketed the countryside, and for the first time in a very long time he was filled with a sense of peace and that all was right in his world. He'd asked himself over and over why he'd survived when Dean hadn't, and he knew it would take time before he would find the answer to that question. He'd come home to heal and reunite with his family, and that was enough.

For now.

Liam saw Harley's reflection in the mirror on the wall in the entryway as he scooped up his phone and a fob off a table. "Sorry, buddy, but you have to stay home tonight," he said in a quiet voice. "I have a date with a pretty girl, and I don't need you to compete with me for her attention. If all goes well tonight and I'm able to have more dates with her, then I will invite her to come to the ranch so that I can properly introduce you to her."

Harley appeared to understand what he'd said when he turned and made his way over to a corner and sat. Liam realized the dog had selected certain areas in the house to claim as his own. Whenever he left the house, it was in the entryway as if to await for his return. Liam had positioned a bed for the dog outside the kitchen, where Harley spent most of his time. The only time he climbed the staircase was before sunrise, and he sat outside Liam's bedroom to wait for him to get up and let him out.

Stetson in hand, Liam walked out of the house and got into the late-model Ram 1500 he'd selected from the garage. He wanted to be early for their date and wait for Charity rather than have her wait for him and wonder if he'd show up.

Liam couldn't recall the last time he'd been to the Tenacity Social Club. Whenever he'd come home on leave it was to sleep around the clock to counter jetlag, then hang out with his brothers to catch up with what had been happening in Tenacity during his absence. He would always visit the stables to reacquaint himself with the horses and occasionally take one out to tour the ranch. There was nothing Liam found more exhilarating than riding horseback while inhaling the smell of freshly mowed grass and the wildflowers dotting the landscape.

That was when he'd been able to commune with everything that made his homecoming so embracing. It just wasn't about the majestic mountains or rivers and streams teeming with fish for fly-fishers. It was also the millions of stars that made it easy to identify different constellations in the nighttime sky. He didn't know why, but it had taken this homecoming for him to realize that he really appreciated Montana's big sky country after being away for prolonged periods of time.

He always knew he would come back to the Double M because it was something he'd promised his father the day before he left for his induction. He'd planned to honorably serve his country for twenty years, then once discharged he would return home and take his place with his brothers to run the ranch. Liam had kept his promise to return to the ranch. Rather than twenty, it had become eight years for him to return home. This time it was to stay.

It was a weeknight, and Liam knew it was easier to find parking than if it had been the weekend. He maneuvered into an empty space behind row of stores, then walked around to the entrance to the Tenacity Social Club. Growing up he'd heard stories that the club located in the basement of a building that also housed the town's post office and barber shop had once been a speakeasy during Prohibition. Once the Volstead Act was repealed it had become a gathering place for locals.

The Social Club was also a place for local Tenacity teenagers to go to during the day to play games on the old-school pinball machines and where Liam and his baseball teammates would always gather after their winning games. There was strict rule that no alcohol would be served to teenagers, but that didn't stop them from getting together in what had become their favorite hangout.

Liam walked in, and it was as if time had stood still. The bar was an old wooden plank with lovers' initials carved into it; there were a number of pinball machines lined against one wall and another covered with flyers advertising math tutoring and other school activities.

He found an empty seat at the bar, and seconds later he was approached by Michael Cooper, who'd earned the reputation of being everyone's favorite bartender. Leaning over the bar, Michael extended his hand.

"Welcome home, Liam. How the hell are you?"

Liam shook the proffered hand. "Right as rain," he said, smiling. He knew if he said it enough, he would come to believe it to be true.

Michael released Liam's hand, then picked up a towel to

wipe down the bar. "I'd heard you were back for good, but I didn't believe it because I know you always talked about becoming a lifer."

Liam nodded. "Life has a way of changing the best-laid plans."

"I know you drink beer, so the first one is on the house."

"Hold up on the beer, because I'm waiting for someone." Less than a second later, he heard a ding on his phone. Charity had sent him a text saying she had to do something first and she hoped to meet him at the Social Club by seven. He returned her text telling her to take her time. She didn't know he'd deliberately gotten there early.

Michael filled a glass with sparkling water, added a slice of lime, then set it on a coaster advertising a popular beer. "Enjoy this until your date gets here," he teased, winking and flashing a Cheshire cat grin.

Liam hadn't had more than a sip of the water when he heard a voice calling out his name and suddenly, he was surrounded by a small crowd as he exchanged handshakes, fist bumps and rough hugs. When asked why he'd left the military he merely said he'd missed his family and Tenacity, and his explanation seemed to satisfy most, though a few had dubious expressions as if they'd known the actual reason why he'd come back home.

He noticed the stares of several men and turned to find Charity John standing a short distance away. Liam's breath caught in his chest. She looked like an angel in a flowing floral blue dress ending mid-thigh that was an exact match for her large luminous eyes. She'd applied a light cover of makeup with muted smokey shades of gray to her eyelids and a rose-pink color on her mouth, and he couldn't believe she could improve on perfection. His gaze moved from her hair flowing in loose waves around her face, over her bared shoulders and down her back. A pair of strappy satin-covered navy-blue stilettos put the top of her head close to his five-ten height.

"Excuse me, gentlemen, but my date is here." Liam bit back a smile when there were murmurs from several men who appeared as if they'd been equally stunned by Charity's natural beauty. Smiling, he reached for Charity's hand, his eyes meeting hers. He dipped his head and kissed her cheek. "You look incredible," he whispered into her ear.

Charity lowered her eyes and smiled. It had taken her more than an hour to select what she'd wanted to wear for her first date with Liam Martin. When she'd packed before leaving Bronco, she'd decided to bring at least a few fancy outfits, unaware that she would be asked out on a date. Jeans and boots had become the norm for her when working at the Double J, but every once in a while, she felt like dressing up, much to her mother's delight. Rather than the Tenacity Social Club, Mimi John would've preferred seeing her daughter married to a wealthy rancher and socializing with other wives at the Association to discuss the latest charity benefit. Still, Charity thought the Social Club charming.

"Thank you," she whispered, inhaling the hypnotic scent of Liam's masculine cologne. He'd exchanged his T-shirt for a starched, white-snapped buttoned shirt, black jeans and matching shiny boots.

Charity's memory of Liam Martin from their meeting the other day paled in comparison to seeing the man face-to-face. His complexion under the Stetson was darker and she attributed that to him spending time in the sun. His large, dark brown penetrating eyes reminded her of cups black coffee with just a splash of cream. And the way he was looking at her made her believe he knew exactly what she thinking and feeling.

Her attraction to Liam had triggered fantasies of his making love to her. She'd tried dismissing them because it had been much too long since she'd been intimate with a man yet knew that was a lie. There was something about Liam when she'd first spied him at Dean's funeral; then again there was another connection when she saw him at the dig.

Charity laced their fingers together. "I hope you didn't have to wait too long for me," she apologized.

"It wouldn't have mattered if you were late because the wait was more than worth it," he said in a quiet voice. Liam released her hand and cradled the small of her back, her muscles jumping before relaxing against his splayed fingers. "I was waiting until you got here to order a drink."

Charity smiled. "I'll have whatever you're drinking." Liam led her to the bar, seating her before claiming the stool next to her. Michael Cooper came over and took their beverage requests, then set out a dish of salty snacks. Less than a minute later, he put two glasses of cold beer on the bar in front of them.

Liam picked up a glass and handed it to her before reaching for his. He touched glasses, smiling. "To new beginnings."

"New beginnings," she repeated, then took a sip of the brew. She gave Liam a sidelong glance at his profile as he drank his beer, and when he turned his head to meet her eyes, a hint of a smile lifted the corners of his mouth. Charity returned the smile. "Should I presume you want to know something about me?" she asked softly.

A low chuckle rumbled in Liam's chest. "I know that

your brother is married to Marisa Sanchez. Are there other Johns I should know about?"

Charity nodded. "I have two more older brothers, Maddox and Jameson."

"So, you're the baby of the family?" he asked.

"Yup."

"Are you close to them?"

"My brothers and I are very tight with one another."

"What about your family? And what do you like to do?"

"My family…" She took another sip of her beer. "Well, let's just say the John family dynamic is…different. My parents are…" Her words trailed off when she realized she was about to share too much for a first date. How could she tell Liam about her parents' reaction to her brothers marrying women who they believed weren't worthy of becoming a John?

"I can't believe I find you so easy to talk to," she said, deftly changing the topic. "It's almost like we've known each other for years," she said with a nervous giggle. "But enough about me. Now it's your turn to tell me about me about you."

Liam knew instinctively that Charity mentioning family dynamics meant the Johns weren't all of one accord, unlike the Martins, who folks claimed were thick as thieves. They never went against one another even if all weren't in agreement. He'd enjoyed listening to Charity, and he was certain he would be able to detect her dulcet voice that was so soothing that he'd found himself completely at ease with her.

"I'm the youngest of three boys. My mother is a retired schoolteacher, and my dad retired from the army with the rank of captain."

"Was your mother an army wife?"

"Yes, but in absentia. Mami refused to live on base with my father."

"Did she live here in Tenacity?"

"Yes. My grandmother looked after me and my brothers until it was time for us to attend school."

"So, you followed your father's footsteps into the military."

Liam nodded. "I served for eight years as a dog handler." He explained he'd been given the responsibility to train military dogs to detect drugs and explosives and also, on command, take down and detain purported perpetrators.

"Do you miss the military?"

It was a question Liam had asked himself once he'd realized his military career was over. "I miss some of my buddies, but what I loved was traveling around the world," he admitted. "Living in the Middle East was an experience I'll never forget. Everything about the awe-inspiring new cities rising from the desert, the food and culture that is so different from ours is what I'd found amazing."

"And you were forced to leave something you love because you were injured."

Liam nodded again. It amazed him how willingly, easily, he told Charity about the injuries he'd sustained when the bomb had accidently exploded and that he'd been in a brain-induced coma for weeks while undergoing surgeries to repair broken bones and skin grafts. "I loved the military as much as I hated being in the hospital. I have to admit that I wasn't a very good patient. But when I think back, I realize I was lucky to get out alive and in one piece. Others weren't as lucky. Once I was stateside, I promised myself that I had to do something to make surviving worthwhile."

He didn't tell Charity that he was seriously thinking about volunteering to talk to high school students about joining the military during career week.

"Have you decided what you'll do next?"

"I'm not sure, except to help my folks around the ranch. Owning and ranching entails nonstop work."

"I didn't know your family owned a ranch."

"The Double M has been in my family for a very long time."

Charity's eyes shimmered like polished blue topaz. "Your family's ranch is the Double M, while my mine is the Double J."

Liam took another sip of beer. "So, you know what it takes to run a ranch." He paused. "What do you do on the Double J?" he questioned.

"I'm responsible for the ranch's digital footprint."

He wasn't certain what Charity meant by a digital footprint but decided to let her talk about the Double J. Liam listened intently when she revealed her family employed a large staff to run a ranch encompassing thousands of acres in Bronco Heights, then it dawned on him that Charity's family was well-to-do.

No, he thought. They weren't just well-to-do. The Johns were filthy rich. Charity spending time in Tenacity was probably like slumming with the less fortunate. He felt a lump in his throat as if he bitten off something too large for him to chew and swallow. What he'd hoped to have with Charity during her stay in Tenacity was over before it was given a chance to begin, because it was apparent they came from very different worlds. A world that was no doubt closed to him and there was his world where she would have a problem becoming accustomed to.

* * *

Charity felt Liam withdraw when she noticed his closed expression. “Did I say something wrong?”

“No.”

“Then why do I feel as if you’re shutting me out?”

“I was just thinking that we come from two very different worlds.”

“You’re not making sense, Liam. We both come from ranching families with a bunch of kids.”

Liam ran a hand over his face. “I don’t want to spoil the evening debating each other.”

“I don’t want to spoil it, either.” She bit her lip. “I want to thank you for listening to me because as the only girl in my family I’m rarely taken seriously. I’m not saying I’m not loved, but I’ve never felt the equal of my brothers. And I’ve dated men who have never been interested in anything I have to say.”

“But you are interesting,” Liam stated.

“And so are you,” Charity countered. “Last year I’d decided to take a break from dating, but when I saw you at Dean’s funeral and saw your eyes—kind and compassionate eyes—I thought I felt a connection. That’s why I agreed to go out with you.” She paused, biting her lip again. “Do you think that’s crazy?”

Liam rested his hand over her smaller one on the bar. “No, it’s not crazy, because when I saw you at the funeral I’d thought about going over to you but realized it would’ve been inappropriate.”

She flashed a bright smile. “Then less than twenty-four hours later, fate brought us back together again!”

He angled his head. “Was it fate or magic?”

“It has to be both, Liam. And I don’t want this to be the last time we see each other.”

* * *

Liam wasn't superstitious, yet he knew something was at play that had brought him and Charity together. He also knew he had to stop questioning why he'd survived the exploding bomb and why Charity John had come into his life when he least expected, because it had been her image that had invaded his last dream, an image that didn't leave him waking up screaming and shaking from the horrors he'd heard and seen before losing consciousness.

"And it won't be," he said, smiling. "After all, we did toast to new beginnings."

"Yes, we did," she said cheerfully.

"Do you mind if we just sit and listen to music for while?"

Charity smiled. "Of course I don't mind."

Forty minutes later Liam left a bill on the bar. It was more than enough to pay for their drinks and leave a generous tip. Cradling Charity's elbow, he helped her off the stool, then looped an arm around her waist.

"Is it okay if I call you about us going out again?" he asked, escorting her up the staircase and out of the building to the street. Despite knowing they came from different worlds, Liam realized he wanted to see Charity again. If only to discover why he'd felt so connected to her.

Charity leaned closer, her shoulder touching his. "Of course it's okay."

Liam walked her to her car. It was a top-of-the line Range Rover. A fitting vehicle for a woman who came from money, he mused. He dropped his arm, cradled her face and pressed a light kiss on her cheek.

"Do you want me to follow you to make certain you get home safe?" he whispered.

Reaching up, Charity held on to his wrists. "No, thank you." She lowered her eyes. "Thank you again for tonight."

"Same here." Liam waited until she drove out of the parking lot before he walked to his vehicle.

Emotions he'd never felt before swept over him as he headed back to the Double M. There were two things he and Charity had in common: Their families were ranchers and they lived in Montana. However, that was where similarities ended. He was an ex-soldier and rancher, while Charity was a poor little rich girl from a world he would never fit in to or could imagine becoming a part of.

However, her beauty notwithstanding, Liam had felt comfortable opening up to her. Even when members of his family had asked him about some of his wounded buddies, he had felt the need to shut them down because it had become a Pandora's box he did not want to reopen.

He'd promised Charity they would go out again, yet he knew whatever they would share had an expiration date. Marisa had mentioned Charity had planned to spend a couple of weeks in Tenacity, and that was enough time for them to enjoy each other's company until she returned to Bronco Heights and the life to which she'd been born.

Harley met him when he opened the door to the cabin, whining that he wanted to go out. Liam removed his boots and stood on the porch to wait for his dog to explore the outdoors. It was another ten minutes before Harley returned and raced inside to his bowl of water. Liam closed and locked the door, set his Stetson on the table in the entry and, carrying his boots, climbed the staircase to the second floor. He lingered long enough to brush his teeth, then took off his clothes and got into bed. In the past he would have liked to stay up late watching television, but now it was as if his body silently communicated its need for more periods of rest in order for him to completely heal.

Liam turned off the bedside lamp, closed his eyes and within minutes fell asleep without the disturbing nightmares jolting him awake. And for the second time since coming home he dreamt of a woman with blond hair and blue eyes. Instead of her reaching out to him, this time she was smiling and whispering that everything was going to be okay. He'd returned her smile, believing he would be okay as long as they were together.

Chapter Four

"Do you want to wait in the truck or come inside with me?" Enzo asked Liam, stopping in the lot behind Strom and Son Feed and Farm Supply.

Tenacity was fortunate to have two feed stores: Tenacity Feed and Seed, owned and run by Mel Hastings, and the former, owned by Nathan and Iris Strom. Jack Martin had made it a practice to patronize both establishments offering rural farm goods and equipment, along with gardening tools and feed for pets, livestock and plumbing and hardware. If you couldn't find what you wanted at one, you would be able to purchase what you needed at the other.

Liam unbuckled his seat belt. "I'll go in with you. I need a tank of propane because I'm planning to do some grilling."

"That's what I'm talking about," Enzo crooned as he shut off the pickup's engine. "I was waiting for you to mention the *G* word."

"I'm sure you were," Liam said, grinning, "because now you can get to eat a steak that doesn't resemble a hockey puck or swim in a puddle of blood on your plate."

Enzo came around the truck and dropped an arm over Liam's shoulders. "We all have our gifts, brother, and grilling happens not to be mine. Now, if you want fried fish, then I'm your man."

Liam had to agree with his brother, because Enzo had become an expert fly-fisherman who would clean his catches, then store them in a freezer chest in his mudroom. Whenever somebody mentioned wanting fish, Enzo would thaw out enough to feed the family, marinate them with what he'd claimed was his secret seasoning, then fire up a backyard fry pot. The fish was usually served with sides of their mother's coleslaw and Mexican street corn. An ice chest filled with beer and homemade lemonade provided liquid refreshment to offset the piquant spices on the fish and corn.

"If that's the case, then I'm going to get two tanks of propane," Liam told Enzo. "We can have a Friday-night fish fry and grilled steaks on Saturday."

He'd mentioned Friday and Saturday because the next day belonged to Maria Martin. It was the day when the entire family sat down together for Sunday dinner. Sundays were even more special whenever her husband had come home on an extended military leave, and now as a security consultant, Jack had made sure an assignment didn't call him away from home on weekends.

Enzo wrapped his arm around Liam's neck. "Sounds good. Why don't you get the tanks while I pick up my order of horse feed?"

Marco and Enzo had decided to give the horses an organic feed made up of oats, peas, alfalfa pellets, barley, kelp and probiotics, and because a few in the herd had come up with digestive issues when fed, corn and soy. Waiting until his eyes adjusted from coming out of bright sunlight Liam came face-to-face with a person he hadn't seen in years.

Smiling, he extended his hand to Caleb Strom. "Hey!

How's it been?" he asked, greeting the man who'd taken over running the business from his semiretired parents.

Caleb ignored Liam's hand and gave him a rough hug. "That's what I should be asking you. I'd heard you were back, but I've been so busy here that I hardly get time to sit down and eat."

Liam pointed to the shiny gold band on the third finger of Caleb's left hand. "Is that all for show?"

Caleb stared at his outstretched fingers. "No, man. It's real. Faith Hawkins and I couldn't decide on a date because we were waiting for a hiatus during the Hawkins Sisters' rodeo schedule so that we could make it a family affair."

"Congratulations to you and your bride." Liam was aware that the name Hawkins was synonymous with rodeo.

"Thanks. Now, what can I help you with?" Caleb asked.

"I need a couple of tanks of propane."

"You came at the right time because I just got in a shipment yesterday. Wait here and I'll get them from the shed and leave them at the front for you."

Liam walked up and down aisles, recalling the times he'd come to the store whenever his father or brothers needed animal feed, fertilizer and/or equipment to dig holes to replace worn or damaged fence posts. Montana winters were beset with blizzards and wind gusts blowing snow into drifts that made driving nearly impossible, along with below-zero temperatures lasting days and occasionally a week or longer. Smiling, he touched the brim of his hat to acknowledge those with whom he'd grown up or who were familiar with his family as he lingered in an aisle to examine a supply of gardening tools.

"Well, as I live and breathe. Liam Martin. Fancy meeting you here."

Liam turned and smiled at Jeanine Hicks, who had been

every high school boy's fantasy and the envy of most girls. She'd been voted prettiest and best dressed in their graduating class because of her delicate features, flawless mahogany complexion and tall, slender figure.

"I could say the same about you, Jeanine. The last I heard you were a flight attendant."

"That's true, but I've decided to take some time off now that I'm married and expecting my first child early next year."

He silently admired her neatly braided hair framing her round face. "Congratulations." It was the second time in a matter of minutes that he'd congratulated somebody in his hometown on their marriage.

Jeanine shyly lowered her eyes. "Thank you. I don't know if you'd heard, but Stuart Ocasio and I decided to live together while he was attending medical school, because I'd been assigned to international flights. Once I discovered I was pregnant, we flew to Vegas to get married, and a week later I resigned from the airline."

Stuart had been one of Liam's baseball teammates and had earned the reputation as an outstanding homerun hitter. A number of Major League Baseball scouts had attended Tenacity's home and away games to watch Stuart, offering him athletic scholarships to attend several colleges, but in the end, he'd turned them down because he wanted to become a doctor.

"Are you guys living in Tenacity?"

Jeanine nodded. "We had an apartment in St. Louis when Stuart attended the Washington University School of Medicine, but we moved back to Tenacity a couple of days ago after Stuart's mother convinced us to move in with her. I believed she didn't like living alone after losing her husband, so in the end everything worked out well for all of us. Stuart just graduated medical school and will intern at a hospital just outside of Billings."

"Good for him."

"If you have the..." Jeanine's words trailed off when a salesperson came over to give her a pair of pruning shears.

"I think this is what you'll need."

Nodding, Jeanine smiled. "Yes, thank you," she said before shifting her attention back to Liam. "I wanted to say now that you're home on leave, you should come and visit us so we can catch up on old times. I know when Stuart has a break he would love to see you again."

Liam didn't tell Jeanine he wasn't on leave because he didn't want to rehash the events which had abruptly upended his life. Each and every time a person asked about what had happened to derail his military career, to him it was like reliving the horrors all over again. The whistling of the bomb before it exploded and then the carnage left in its wake. Liam was still struggling with wanting to feel comfortable socializing with other people who went about their regular lives without missing a beat. Meanwhile, he woke each morning knowing what he could and could not do. Going on a date with Charity had gone surprisingly well because he was aware that her time in Tenacity had an expiration date. And when that time came, she would go back to Bronco Heights and the Double J, while he would continue to live and work on the Double M in Tenacity.

"Please let Stuart know I'll be in touch now that I know you guys are living with his mother."

"Will do," Jeanine said. "I'm planning to prune Stuart's mother's garden, so I want to get back and start working before it gets too hot."

Liam huffed a breath of relief when Jeanine headed to the front of the store to pay for her gardening tool. When

Enzo asked if he wanted to accompany him to the feed store, Liam hadn't hesitated, because he needed to see more than the Double M. When he'd gone to the Society Club the night before it was akin to going back to when he was in high school and would hang out there with his classmates. They would order pop, challenge one another when playing pinball and just do and say things they wouldn't when around their parents.

Most of the kids had paired off into couples by the time he'd entered high school, but it had been different for Liam. Rather than date, he'd joined a number of other boys and girls who'd preferred to remain unencumbered. Stuart had confided to him that he'd had a crush on Jeanine but that she'd refused to go out with him because he was a jock. Jock notwithstanding, Stuart was a brilliant student who was the valedictorian of their graduating class. Stuart had achieved his dream of becoming a doctor while the girl he'd fantasized about became his wife.

However, now things were different for Liam. He was no longer an adolescent boy with a dream of making the military his career. He had no high school girlfriend to return to and pick up where they'd left off. He was more than grateful that he had his parents, brothers, Harley and the Double M.

He returned to the front of the store where Enzo had stacked two fifty-pound bags of feed on a flatbed dolly along with the tanks of propane. Reaching into his pocket, Liam took out his phone to pay for their purchase, but then his brother stopped him.

"Just pay for the propane," Enzo said. "The feed is charged to the ranch's account," he explained, handing the salesperson a credit card stamped with *Double M, Inc.*

It was apparent Jack Martin sought to keep the family's

personal expenses separate from those required to operate the ranch. Liam paid for the propane and walked out with Enzo pushing the cart to the pickup. The instant he'd attempted to take the bag of feed off the cart he felt a slight cramp in his shoulders. The dull pain was a constant reminder that even after hours of rehab to regain range of motion, he had to be careful not to overdo it.

Enzo tossed him the fob. "You can drive back. I'll finish loading everything. And please don't argue with me, Liam, because I saw your face when you tried lifting the bag of feed. Despite what you'd like to believe, you're not an indestructible superhero. You forget I was in that VA hospital where you were covered with bandages and had machines monitoring your vitals. It was also the first time I saw our father cry. And if you ever mention to him that I told you, I will beat the hell out of you."

"And what do you think Harley would do if you did attempt to hit me?" he asked, biting back a smile. "My partner would rip you to shreds."

Bending slightly from the knees, Enzo effortlessly picked up the bag of feed and set it in the truck. "What you need is a partner with two, not four, legs."

A slight frown furrowed Liam's forehead. "What are you talking about?"

"A woman, bro! It's time you go out and have some fun with some pretty young woman. The Double M will be here when we're old and gray."

Liam wanted to tell Enzo he'd found a pretty young woman but whatever fun they would have wouldn't last more than a couple of weeks before she had to return to Bronco. "I'll think about it."

"Do more than think about it, Liam. Just do it!"

"Who are you, Enzo, a spokesperson for the Nike brand?"

Enzo cut his eyes at him. "Very funny," he drawled. He got into the truck and slammed the passenger door.

"I don't know why you're so revved up on me getting involved with a woman when you could've married and made our mother an *abuela*."

"That's a long story," Enzo said, staring out the windshield as Liam drove away from the feed store.

"Do you want to tell me about it?"

Enzo shook his head. "Nah, bro. It's something I'd promised myself I never wanted to talk about again."

"That bad?"

"It was really bad," Enzo confirmed. "At least it was for me," he added after a noticeable silence.

Liam concentrated on driving. It was apparent his brother had had his heart broken, while he'd been exempt for loving and losing. He wasn't anti-marriage, yet knew he wasn't ready to settle down with a woman at this time in his life. The past six months had made him aware of his mortality, and because he'd been given a second chance at life, he planned to make everything he did meaningful. While his decision to date Charity during her stay in Tenacity was a hint of what he could possibly experience with a woman in the future.

He drove through the entrance to the ranch, stopping at the barn where he'd left his pickup. Liam set one tank of propane on the floor behind the front seat, then drove back to his cabin where Harley got up from where he'd been sleeping on the porch.

"Hey, buddy. After I put away the propane, I'll take you out where you can play with your new friends."

Liam had come to enjoy watching Harley chase the

three herding dogs, growling and nipping playfully until he clapped his hands to get the shepherd's attention. It was the signal for him to stop and come over and sit beside him.

He stored the propane in a corner of the patio at the rear of the cabin not far from a waterproof-covered gas grill. Whenever he'd returned to the Double M on leave, Liam preferred cooking on the grill rather than turn on the oven in his kitchen. Like most ranching families, children who grew up on the ranch were gifted with their own cabins on the property where they could live and raise the next generation of Martins. His cabin, Marco's and Enzo's were constructed far enough from one another and the main house to ensure complete privacy. And, unlike his brothers, he had never invited a woman to come spend the night because not only hadn't he dated anyone in Tenacity, but whenever he'd come home on leave, he'd wanted to spend all of his time with his family.

Liam opened the rear door to the pickup and waited for Harley jumped in. He closed the door and got in behind the wheel and headed in the direction of the property where several herds were grazing. His father had made certain to move the herds around the ranch to prevent overgrazing. Harley stood up when he saw the cattle and as soon as Liam came to a stop and opened the door, he jumped out and sprinted to where the herding dogs were.

Liam sat on the ground, supporting his back against the truck's bumper, then opened the top of a travel mug and took a long swallow of water. He pulled his Stetson lower on his forehead and closed his eyes. He lost track of time unaware he'd fallen asleep until Harley came and nudged him with his nose.

Pushing to his feet, he waited for Harley to get into the vehicle before reversing direction and driving home.

* * *

"If I didn't see that tag hanging over the rim, I would've thought that you were trying to read tea leaves the way you've been staring into that cup."

Charity's head popped when she heard Marisa's voice. "I'm sorry, but I didn't hear you come in." She'd overslept that morning, something she rarely did. Her movements had been slow when she'd showered, gotten dressed, then gone into the kitchen to brew a cup of tea rather than her usual coffee.

Marisa ran her fingers through the hair on her nape as she sat down at the table across from her sister-in-law. "What's bothering you?"

Charity's blue eyes met a dark brown pair, the color reminding her of Liam's. "Why do you believe something's bothering me?"

"It's not a something, Charity."

"If it's not a something, then who or what is it?" Charity asked, her voice rising slightly in frustration. Marisa was talking in riddles, while she couldn't stop thinking about Liam. His reference to them coming from two different worlds had kept her from a restful night's sleep.

"The who is Liam Martin," Marisa said, giving her a direct stare. "I know you went out with him last night, but you came home much earlier than I'd expected. Did the two of you have a fight?"

"No, we didn't have a fight."

"Then why the long face?" Marisa questioned.

Charity huffed. "It was something Liam said that is bothering me."

Marisa leaned forward. "What did he say?"

"He said something about us coming from different worlds."

A frown appeared between Marisa's eyes. "What did he mean by that?"

Charity shook her head. "I don't know. I told him he wasn't making sense because we both come from ranching families."

"What did he say after that?"

"He claimed he didn't want to argue with me and spoil what had been a really nice night for him."

"How about you, Charity? Did you have a nice time with him?"

"Of course I did. He's the first man I've met who seemed genuinely interested in what I had to say. And please don't tell me he was just being polite."

"I grew up and went to school with Liam, and I can honestly say he is one of the nicest guys I've ever known. He was into sports, but he wasn't the typical jock. There was never any talk about him trying to hit on girls who were willing to sleep around."

This disclosure about a younger Liam roused Charity's curiosity. "Was it because he had a steady girlfriend?"

"No."

"Are you saying he didn't like girls?"

Marisa gave Charity an incredulous stare. "You mean… No, not at all. He liked girls, but since he planned to enlist right after graduation, he didn't want to ask some girl to wait around for him."

Charity had to respect Liam for that. "So, he's never dated a girl from Tenacity?"

"He's dating you," Marisa answered smugly.

"But I'm not from Tenacity," Charity countered.

"You could be if you moved to the ranch with me and Dawson."

Charity slowly shook her head. "I can't do that. I'm responsible for the Double J's digital footprint."

"That's something you can do remotely, Charity. And Bronco is less than two hours away, so you can always drive back several times a week."

Seconds ticked into a full minute before Charity said, "Why are you trying so hard to get me and Liam together?"

"Because Liam has been through a lot and he needs someone like you, who won't cause him any unnecessary angst. I don't think you realize that you would be perfect for him."

"It seems as if you have a lot of faith in me. And remember I'm only going to be in Tenacity for a couple of weeks."

"I have a lot of faith in you because I love you like a sister."

"That goes double for me," Charity said, grinning. She wanted to tell Marisa about the connection she'd felt when she first saw Liam at Dean's funeral and then again at the dig, but decided it was too soon to reveal her feelings about a strange man who had come into her life when she'd sworn off dating anyone because none of the men have taken her seriously or treated her as an independent woman.

"Are you going to go out with him again?"

Charity's cell dinged before she could answer Marisa's question. Glancing at the phone next the cup, she saw Liam's name. He'd sent her a text. "Excuse me, but I need to respond to this," she said, reading what he'd sent her. He was asking if she would be willing to go to lunch with him around one the following afternoon. "Liam wants me to go on a picnic with him tomorrow."

"Tell him yes!" Marisa shouted at her.

She typed yes, adding a smiley face. Liam replied with one blowing a kiss. Leaning over the table, she showed

Marisa the phone. "To answer your question…yes, I'm going out with him again."

"That's my girl."

Charity wanted to tell Marisa that she was reading too much into her sharing a picnic lunch with Liam. Just because she'd found her happily-ever-after with Dawson, it didn't translate into Charity achieving the same with Liam. He'd come home as a vet who'd sustained injuries serious enough where he was no longer fit for duty. She knew that had to be devastating for someone who'd planned to make the military his career to abruptly have to shift back to civilian life

That was the same thing Dean had talked about when they were dating. That he couldn't wait to enlist and become a soldier responsible for serving and protecting his country. There were times when Charity believed he'd become so obsessed with everything military that it had become the sole focus of their conversations. He'd fulfilled his passion because not only had he become a soldier, he'd died honorably, serving his country.

Pushing back her chair, Charity got up and emptied the remains of the cold tea into the sink, rinsed the cup and put it in the dishwasher. "What's on your agenda today?" she asked Marisa.

"I thought about driving out to the ranch to see if the renovations on the main house are near completion, because I'm more than ready to move in before next month."

"Give me a few minutes to put my hair up, and I'll go with you." Going out to the ranch would become a welcome distraction from her sitting around thinking about Liam. Even if those thoughts were good ones.

Chapter Five

"Are you going to tell me the name of the young lady you're planning to take out on a picnic?" Liam's mother asked him as he continued to fill a large wicker hamper with the containers of salads and desserts he'd asked her to help him prepare. "She must be very special because it's been a while since I've been asked to make a Waldorf salad."

"Her name is Charity John, Mami."

"John," Maria whispered. "Why does that name sound so familiar?"

"It's because her brother is married to Marisa Sanchez."

Maria clapped a hand over her mouth. "Aren't they the Johns from Bronco Heights?"

"Yup," Liam confirmed. He tightened the caps on bottles of chilled water, cranberry lemonade and iced tea and set them in a corner of the basket with several cool packs.

Maria removed the bandana covering her salt-and-pepper hair and met Liam's eyes. "You just got back, so how do you know this girl?"

"She used to date a guy who was in my unit. Unfortunately, he died from the injuries he'd sustained when the bomb exploded."

"You're dating a dead man's girlfriend?"

Liam halted filling the basket and gave his mother a long, penetrating stare. "It's not like that."

"Then tell me what it's like," Maria said, fluidly switching to Spanish.

Liam was aware whenever his mother spoke Spanish it was because she was frustrated or upset. "I saw her for the first time at the military funeral for Dean Valentini the day I came home. Then I saw her the next day at the dinosaur dig, and after Marisa introduced us, she told me that she had dated Dean but they parted as friends."

Maria narrowed her eyes. "And how do you see her, Liam?"

He closed and latched the top of the basket. "Charity is a friend and nothing more than that. She's only going to be in Tenacity for a couple of weeks before she has to go back to Bronco."

"Is she pretty?"

Liam slowly shook his head. "What's up with the interrogation, Mami? I know you want your sons to settle down with women and give your grandchildren, but that's not going to happen with me and Charity. And I know what you're thinking. There's no future with me and Charity because we're going to keep it light and enjoy each other's company before she returns home."

"So, you plan to date her while she's here visiting with her family?"

"If not date, then see her whenever she's not busy. It's not as if she's waiting around for me to call her, Mami."

"You realize this is the first time you've ever taken out a woman who lives in Tenacity."

"Visiting Tenacity, Mami."

Maria waved her hand. "Visiting, living. It's all the same."

"Yeah, yeah," Liam drawled. Walking over to his mother, he kissed her cheek. "Thanks for all your help."

Maria rested a hand on his clean-shaven jaw. "Anytime. My door is open if you wish to bring your *friend* to eat with us."

"I'll let you know," he said noncommittally, because he'd changed his mind about bringing Charity to the ranch. Bringing her to the Double M and introducing her to his family could possibly send the wrong message, and Liam didn't want to lead Charity on or fool his family into believing something that was impossible. He didn't want to plan a future with Charity or expose her to the horrific nightmares that had become his personal prison.

Charity was waiting for Liam when he drove up to the Sanchez house at one. Smiling and cradling several blankets to her chest, she met him when he came around to open the passenger door for her. He'd chosen a perfect day for an outdoor picnic. Midday temperatures peaked in the low eighties with cooling mountain breezes offsetting the blinding rays of the sun in a cloudless sky.

Staring, she took in everything about Liam in one sweeping glance from his black straw Stetson, black body-hugging T-shirt accentuating bulging biceps, slim-cut black jeans and matching boots. His cologne, a blend of sandalwood and lime, matched perfectly with his body's natural pheromones. There was something so overwhelmingly masculine about Liam Martin dressed entirely in black that wouldn't allow Charity to look away, and she was glad that she was wearing sunglasses so he wouldn't see her eyes figuratively eating him up.

Smiling, Liam took the blankets from her. "I should've told you that I was bringing blankets."

"Do you want me to take them back into the house?"

"No. I'll put them in the truck with the others."

Liam cradled her elbow, assisting her as she climbed up into the Ram that still had a new-car smell. Charity secured her seat belt, took off her hat, then stretched out her legs. He'd left the engine running, and the song "Rumor" filled the vehicle's interior. Closing her eyes, she sang along with the chorus, her perfect-pitched melodious voice blending with Lee Brice's soulful rendition of his country hit.

Liam slipped in behind the wheel, then went completely still when he heard Charity singing along with a tune he'd downloaded on his phone's playlist. He'd liked the song the first time he'd heard it, but now, listening to Charity's singing, the lyrics took on a new meaning. And because they were seen together at the Social Club, there was no doubt Tenacity's rumor mill would go into overdrive about his dating a girl in his little town.

"Wow!" he whispered when the song ended. "You were incredible. I had no idea you could sing like that."

Charity removed her glasses and lowered her eyes, seemingly embarrassed by his compliment. "Thank you."

"No, thank you," Liam countered. "Your voice is incredible."

"I have Marisa to thank for giving me the confidence I needed to believe in myself."

"It was more than obvious that she did a masterful job. When did she tutor you?"

"Two years ago. She'd been hired to organize and direct Bronco's annual Mistletoe Pageant at the Bronco Theater. I'd asked Dawson to go to the audition with me for moral support, because I was a total fangirl of Marisa after one of her TikTok videos went viral. I'd always loved singing, but I didn't believe I had the talent to perform in front of an audience."

"Should I assume the pageant was a rousing success?" Liam asked, backing out of the driveway.

"It was incredible, and I got to believe in my talent. I wasn't the only John to become a winner, though, because Dawson and Marisa had fallen in love with each other."

"What made you think you weren't born with an incredible talent? It may sound clichéd, but your voice is a gift from the gods."

She smiled. "You have to know that you're good for a woman's ego."

Liam took his eyes off the road to shoot Charity a quick glance. "I've never been one to stroke a woman's ego and tell her what she wants or needs to hear."

"That's something I can really appreciate. However, I'd like for you to answer one question for me."

"Only one question?" Liam teased, smiling.

Charity also smiled. "One for now. In my past…well… What I don't understand is why men say things to women they don't believe themselves."

Liam chuckled. "That's something I can't answer, because my father lectured me and my brothers over and over that trust is the most important component in a relationship. Once trust is broken things will never be the same."

"If more men were like your father, I believe there would be fewer breakups in marriages or relationships."

"True, but there are some situations where couples are better off apart than together."

"Are you speaking from experience, Liam?" Charity asked.

Liam wasn't certain whether he wanted to tell Charity about some of the women with whom he'd been involved, because none had progressed to the stage where marriage had become a topic of conversation.

"Yes," he admitted after a pregnant pause.

"Did she break your heart?"

"No, Charity, she didn't break my heart because it never got to the point where we were that involved with each other." He met her eyes briefly when she shifted to stare at him. "She was a civilian and I was being transferred to a different base, so we both knew seeing each other had an expiration date. What about you, Charity? Were you ever a member of the broken-hearts club?"

"I can honestly say no. But I did date this guy, Nick, casually for a while, but it didn't work out. I know my mother was very disappointed when we broke up, but I couldn't convince myself that he was someone I wanted to settle down with."

"Could it be because you were fickle?" he teased.

"Funny you would say that, because that's what my brothers were saying about me. I was all of twenty, and at that age I had a right to be fickle."

"What about now, Charity? Are you still fickle at the ripe old age of twenty-four?" Liam teased.

"No. Because now I know what I want and don't want," she countered.

"And what's that?"

"To control my own destiny. I intend to do what makes me happy and fulfilled."

"Do you think that's possible?" Liam asked. He'd wanted to remind Charity that not only was she the youngest in the family, she was the only girl, and as a Bronco Heights John she had a certain standard to live up to.

"Yes, it's possible." She paused. "Do you realize we just

passed the road leading to your ranch?" There were markers along the roads in Tenacity identifying many of the ranches.

Liam nodded. "Yes, because we're not going to my ranch."

"Where are we going?"

"Someplace where I used to hang out when I was in high school. During the summer kids would pile into pickups and drive to an area above a valley where you could see for miles. It was far enough from town and the prying eyes of adults, so kids could do things they didn't want their parents to see."

She gave him a side glance. "Like make out, smoke and drink?" she teased.

"No comment," Liam replied.

Charity rested her hand on his right one on the wheel. "Are you admitting to being a naughty boy?"

"No," he answered truthfully. "My badass military father warned me and my brothers that if we were ever picked up for underage drinking and smoking, then we would be confined to the ranch until we were old enough to go off on our own."

"What about school?"

"My mother was a teacher, so she would've assumed the responsibility of homeschooling us."

"So, in other words, y'all were scared straight?"

"We were until we became teenagers, then we realized most times Dad was just blowing smoke. It's Maria Martin who is one tough lady and who had to hold it down and keep her family together raising three boys while her military husband was away."

"Tell me about your family, Liam."

He decelerated and came to a stop in a wooded area

where the landscape sloped down into a valley. "What do you want to know?" he asked Charity.

"Everything."

"Everything?"

Charity flashed a white-toothed smile. "Everything you're willing to disclose. And I promise not to pump you to reveal family secrets."

Liam shut off the Ram's engine and undid his seat belt, then turned to give Charity a direct stare, silently admiring the length of her long dark lashes. "The Martins aren't hiding any secrets. In our closets we don't have skeletons of horse thieves, cattle rustlers, bank, train and stagecoach robbers like some folks around these parts."

"A lot of those people were the ones who'd help settle this part of the country," Charity said in a quiet voice.

His eyebrows lifted slightly, and Liam wondered if past generations of Johns were guilty of taking advantage of small ranchers or farmers to amass their wealth. "Settled to become rich and powerful."

Vertical lines appeared over the bridge of Charity's straight nose. "Not all families accrue wealth through illegal or unethical means."

Liam angled his head. "There's no need to get upset, Charity. I didn't mention your family."

"No, but—"

"I invited you to go out with me," he said, interrupting her, "not to argue, but to enjoy the day and each other," he added, smiling and hoping to diffuse a debate on a topic which would end without a winner or loser. The state's history books were filled with stories of Montana range wars and violent conflicts primarily between sheep and cattle ranchers over grazing rights during the late nineteenth and early twentieth centuries. Some of his ancestors had become collateral damage during the range wars when a group of wealthy cattlemen had driven his sheep-raising family off their land. It had taken several generations of Martins working for other ranchers and farmers to save enough money to purchase land and establish their own ranch.

Charity's mouth slowly curved into a smile. "Fine with me. I don't know what you've packed in that basket, but I'm ready to get my eat on."

"Please wait in the truck while I get the blankets and unpack everything."

"Why do I have to wait?"

"Because I'm going to try and find a shady spot under some trees so you won't end up looking like a cooked lobster."

She extended her arms. "I put on sunblock on my face, and I'm also wearing a hat and a shirt with long sleeves, so I'm good."

"If that's the case, then you can help me." Liam got out, came around the pickup and extended his hand to help Charity down. She smiled up at him, and Liam was unable to look away. He didn't know what there was about Charity John that had him reacting like a middle school boy crushing on a girl who would pass him in the halls as if he didn't exist. She'd talked about fate bringing them together, and inasmuch as he hadn't wanted to believe it, he realized she was right. Standing mere inches apart, inhaling the scent of her perfume and noticing the tenderness in her gaze filled him with a gentle peace that had evaded him for months. She lowered her eyes, shattering the spell she unknowingly had woven over him.

Lacing their fingers together, he led her over to an area where a copse of low-hanging trees provided a modicum of shade, at least until the sun's direction shifted later that afternoon.

"What do you think?" he asked Charity.

"It's perfect. I'll lay out the blankets while you get the basket."

Charity sat back on her sock-covered feet after she'd removed her hat and boots, watching Liam unload the picnic basket with glass containers filled with what she'd thought of as a smorgasbord of delicious goodness.

"What on earth did you pack?" she asked, watching as he uncovered the containers. "It looks as if you bought out everything in a gourmet shop."

Liam's head popped up. "Tenacity doesn't have a gourmet shop. What you see is compliments of the Martin family kitchen."

She gave him a wide-eyed stare. "You had your mother cook all of this?" There were containers of guacamole, deviled eggs, Waldorf, Greek, and potato salads, coleslaw and tabbouleh.

"My mother made the Waldorf and potato salads and slaw. I made everything else."

Charity slowly blinked. "You cook." The question came out like a statement.

Smiling and nodding, Liam, said, "My mother taught all her sons to cook." He handed Charity a plate and place setting wrapped in a cloth napkin. "Dig in and take whatever you like."

Charity filled her plate with Waldorf salad, a deviled egg topped with spinach and bacon, guacamole and tabbouleh. She met Liam's eyes when he stared at her plate. "This is just my first course." She planned to sample everything Liam had packed for their picnic lunch.

"Eat as much as you want, because I don't intend to bring home leftovers."

Charity chewed and swallowed a mouthful of Waldorf salad, her eyes widening in shock. It was better than what the chefs at the Association prepared. "Oh my gosh!"

Liam's forkful of tabbouleh halted midair. "What's the matter?"

"The Waldorf salad."

"What about it?"

"It's the best I've ever eaten. And I've ordered it enough whenever I have lunch at the Association."

"Is the Association a restaurant in Bronco?" he questioned.

She shook her head. "No. It's a private club for Bronco Heights ranchers." Within seconds of her explanation, Charity felt a chill sweep over her body and it had nothing to do with the weather. There wasn't a hint of warmth in Liam's dark brown eyes as he looked at her. "Did I say something wrong?" she asked, chiding herself for sounding like a child questioning parents to gain their approval.

"No, Charity," Liam said, his voice void of emotion. "I asked a question, and you answered it for me."

"Why do I feel as if you didn't like my answer?"

He continued to stare at her, making her more and more uncomfortable with each passing second.

"I like you," he said quietly, after a swollen pause. "In fact, I like you a lot, but what I don't want to do is argue and debate things on which we'll never agree. The past six months I went to hell and back, and once I walked out of that last hospital, I promised myself that I would avoid conflict when and wherever possible. And that includes verbal or physical confrontations. Right now, I'm in a dark place and I don't want to bring you into it with me, especially if you've never known what that's like and I pray you'll never have to."

Charity recoiled as if she'd been struck across the face. She wanted to tell Liam he was wrong if he believed she liked arguing because she'd had enough of that with her parents—her mother, in particular, when it came to the men she'd wanted to date. And when he'd mentioned being hospitalized, she knew he'd endured not only physical trauma but emotional as well.

Shifting closer to Liam, Charity wrapped her arms around his neck. "The last thing I want to do is fight with you," she whispered. "You are the most amazing man I've ever met, and whenever I'm with you I feel alive and invincible." She wanted to tell Liam that being with him gave her the confidence she needed to take complete control of her life. With or without the approval of her parents. He treated her like an adult and not someone who didn't have the wherewithal to determine what she wanted for her future.

Smiling, Liam rested his hand alongside her jaw. "In case you don't know it, you're pretty amazing yourself, Charity John."

"Really?"

He nodded. "Yes, really."

"I think I'm going to need some convincing," she whispered.

Charity felt as if everything around her was moving in slow motion when Liam eased her down to the blanket, his body covering hers. Then his head came down, breathing in her breath before his mouth caressed her parted lips.

She felt as if she was floating, higher than she ever been before because no man had ever kissed her with a combination of tenderness and passion, arousing her to where she wanted to beg him to strip her naked and make love to her where they lay.

Liam ended the kiss, and Charity buried her face against his neck. "Do you really think we should be doing this?" she said breathlessly.

"Do what?"

"I have a hard-and-fast rule to never kiss on the first date."

He laughed softly. "This happens to be our second date. Remember our first one was at the Social Club?"

"If that's the case, I wouldn't mind if you kiss me again," she teased, smiling.

Reaching up, Liam gently removed her arms from his neck. "I think we should finish our lunch before we end up doing something I don't think either of us is ready for."

Charity knew he was right. Although she wanted to experience making love with Liam, she had to be realistic. She'd planned to stay in Tenacity for two weeks, and that wasn't enough time for her to have a meaningful relationship with a man. Especially with one who'd made it clear that he didn't want a relationship. Even one with whom she was experiencing a connection so strong it was frightening.

Liam rolled off Charity, and she was able to put a modicum of comfortable space between them. She picked up her plate to begin eating again. After seconds, she put down her fork and touched a napkin to the corners of her mouth.

"We did good," Liam said. "There're hardly any leftovers."

"That's because everything was scrumptious. I wouldn't mind if you cooked for me every day."

Liam knew cooking for Charity meant her coming to his cabin on the Double M. But he didn't want to give her the wrong idea. He and Charity John were friends, and at this point in his life he could not envision them crossing the line to lovers. He was damaged goods, unfit for duty and suffering from PTSD. He didn't want Charity or any woman to witness the frightening nightmares that had left him shaking and screaming uncontrollably.

Then he recalled his mother saying, *My door is open if you wish to bring your friend to eat with us.* Liam didn't want to read more into Maria Martin's invitation. He'd suspected his mother was curious to meet the woman who'd gotten her youngest son interested enough in her to openly date in Tenacity.

"What if I asked you to cook for me?" He paused. "That is, if you can cook."

"I can cook," Charity said defensively.

"What you would make?"

"It would depend on whether it would be breakfast, lunch or dinner."

"Oh, it's like that?" Liam teased, grinning. "What would you prepare for breakfast?"

Sitting back on the heels, Charity tucked a strand of sun-bleached hair behind an ear. "I'm partial to omelets, eggs Benedict, steak and eggs, and chicken and waffles. It was different in college, but that's something I'll explain at another time."

"That sounds more than brunch than breakfast," Liam countered.

"It's because I prefer eating brunch to an American or continental breakfast. Lunch would usually be a salad with lots of greens, veggies and occasionally protein like chicken or shrimp." She paused. "I always order the Waldorf salad at the Association. Their Ceasar salad is always prepared tableside, and there's also the aged premium steaks at Coeur de l'Ouest in Bronco Heights where you have to make reservations weeks in advance."

He thought about her comparing his mother's Waldorf salad to the one she'd ordered at the private country club for wealthy Bronco ranchers. And her reference to a restaurant where there was a waitlist for reservations made the differences between them even more obvious that again it was an indication that they'd come from different worlds. The only common thread was both families were ranchers.

"What about dinner?" he asked.

Charity huffed. "Dinner is usually meat, carbs, with soup or salad, and always with dessert. If or when I ever cook for you, then you'd have to let me know what you don't like or are allergic to."

"I can't eat raw fish." He'd sampled sushi and quickly discovered it would his first and last time ordering it.

"The first time I had ahi tuna with avocado, tropical salsa sriracha and wasabi I embarrassed myself because I'd requested two orders of it in lieu of an entrée."

"It was that good?"

Charity closed her eyes and ran her tongue over her lower lip. She opened her eyes. "It ranks close to the top of my list of favorite dishes. It's not that I don't appreciate steak or barbecue ribs, but sushi and sashimi are a welcome departure from red meat."

"Even though we are in cattle country, the rivers and streams in Montana are filled with wild trout if you like fish," Liam reminded Charity.

"True, but whenever I go to restaurants in Bronco, I rarely order fish. By the way, do you fly-fish?" Charity asked him.

"No. My brother Enzo is an expert fly-fisherman."

"Have you tried fishing?" she asked.

Nodding, Liam smiled. "Several times, but I was never able to catch anything."

"I don't have the patience to stand in nearly waist-deep in water waiting for a fish to bite."

Liam laughed softly. "That's something we can both agree on. Are you ready to go back?" he asked as Charity stared at something over his shoulder.

"Not yet. That is if you don't have something to do."

"I don't. We can hang out here a little longer."

She smiled. "I'd like that."

Chapter Six

They'd cleared away the remains from the picnic, packing everything into the hamper, then lay side by side together on the blanket. Charity smiled when Liam reached for her hand and laced their fingers together. His calloused palms were a welcome change from the smooth ones of some of the men she'd dated. There was so much she wanted to know about this enigmatic stranger with whom she'd wanted to spend every second, minute and hour of her time in Tenacity.

He'd projected a zen calmness, then without warning he would give her look that made her feel as if he was shutting her out. At first, she'd thought it was her imagination. But it'd happened again when she'd mentioned the Association. She didn't know why his reference to their coming from different worlds continued to nag at her, shattering any confidence she had that she could possibly have an ongoing relationship with Liam Martin. It didn't matter that he lived in Tenacity and she in Bronco. If Dawson was able to have a relationship with Marisa, then it was possible for her and Liam. But then she recalled his telling her he was in a dark place and she wondered if that was the reason why he was reluctant to allow her to get close to him. What Liam didn't know was that she was willing to wait for him to emerge from that dark place where they could have a relationship and could meet on equal footing.

Turning her head, she stared at his profile. "Tell me more about the Martins," she said after a prolonged silence.

"What do you want to know?"

"When did they first settle Montana?"

Liam huffed an audible breath. "I've heard stories about some of my ancestors who'd served as Colored Troops during the Civil War. A few stayed in the military joining Buffalo Soldier units. They served in the westward expansion, patrolling the frontier, building infrastructure and were involved in fighting major campaigns against Native American tribes."

"Was it their military service that was responsible for them moving west?"

Liam nodded. "Serving in the army allowed them the opportunity to escape the restrictive laws of the Black Codes that were passed in the Southern states after the Civil War and the abolition of slavery. Once they were discharged some went to California, others traveled to Oregon and Washington to work as loggers, while my third-generation great-grandfather, Lemuel Martin, came to Montana and found work as a horse wrangler. He saved his money, bought some land, married a young Indigenous woman, and together they had a lot of children. There were rumors passed down through the family that he didn't regret being a soldier but was consumed with guilt because he'd been ordered to hunt down and kill Native Americans who were fighting to keep their sacred tribal lands. The very people whose blood ran in the veins of his children."

"What did he do once he bought land?" Charity asked.

"He became a sheep and goat farmer. However, it wasn't

a good time to raise sheep because cattlemen were buying up huge tracts of land to graze large herds of cattle. I'm certain you've read about Montana range wars and violent conflicts primarily between sheep and cattle ranchers over grazing rights during the late nineteenth and early twentieth centuries. He was forced to sell his livestock and eventually moved his family to a region close to what would eventually become Tenacity.

"There were great herds of wild horses on federal land, and the government gave settlers permission to round them up rather than have them hunted and slaughtered like the buffalo. That's when the Martins set up a horse ranch and years later were responsible for selling horses and mules to the army during World War I.

"It wasn't until after the Great Depression that they'd finally decided raise beef cattle. They started with Herefords, then added Angus. My grandfather crossbred an Angus bull with several Santa Gertrudis cows which added invaluable traits for both breeds. Santa Gertrudis have the ability to thrive in various climates, and the quality of their meat produces very little fat."

"Do you still raise both breeds?" Most ranchers she knew favored one breed.

"Yes."

"Why not one or the other?" she questioned.

"Santa Gertrudis happen to be one of the world's leading producers of quality meat. The cows have easy birthing because their calves have smaller birth weight, but pack on the pounds when weaned. Santas are one of the leading cattle breeds in Australia, while the King Ranch in Texas is renowned for the development of the breed."

Charity wanted to visit the Double M to see the Martin's cattle. "Do you like being a rancher?"

* * *

Liam closed his eyes and smiled. Charity was asking him a question he'd asked himself over and over. Why had he left ranching life on the Double M and enlisted? Was it because he'd become disenchanted working a cattle ranch in a small town that had become a dot on the map? A struggling dot, at that. Or was it the stories he'd heard about generations of Martin men leaving home to serve in the military?

He shrugged. "It's a part of my family's legacy I've promised to uphold," he said truthfully.

"That's not really answering my question."

Liam released her hand, then turned on his side to face her, their noses mere inches apart. "Ranching is in my DNA. And, I guess, I could say the same about the military. When Lemuel Martin donned the uniform of the Union Army to fight in the Civil War, his children and grandchildren were presented with opportunities that had been denied him. They were able marry whomever they loved, purchase land, become farmers, then ranchers. The Double M is home, and it is where I plan to spend the rest of my life." He paused. "I hope that answers your question."

Charity lowered her eyes, long dark lashes resting on high cheekbones. "It does."

"Good."

"Can you answer one more question for me?" she asked.

Liam's eyebrows lifted questioningly. "Only one?" A rush of pink stained her cheeks with his jibe.

"Yes, and I promise not to ask another one. How did the Double M get its name?"

"That's an easy one to answer. There are twins in the Martin family every other generation. Therefore, Double M."

Rising slightly on an elbow, Charity looked at him as if was teasing her. "You're kidding, aren't you?"

Liam smiled. "That's another question, and no, I'm not kidding. It skipped my generation, but there's no doubt there will be twin births if and when my brothers decide to become fathers."

"What about you, Liam? Why aren't you counting yourself in that equation?"

His smile grew wider as he ran a forefinger down the bridge of her nose. "I think you missed your calling, beautiful. You should've been a journalist because you're full of questions."

"That's because I want to know as much as I can about the man I happen to like a lot," she said.

For a prolonged moment Liam continued to study the face of the woman that had him wondering why he'd continued to ignore the silent voice telling him to stay away. That if they were to become involved it would lead to disappointment and eventual heartache.

It wasn't only that they came from different worlds, but he couldn't allow her into his because he feared if she ever witnessed him reliving a nightmare it would leave her traumatized and in fear of her life. It wasn't only the nightmares, but the overall darkness that continued to haunt him.

"I don't want you to like me a lot," he said in a quiet voice.

Charity slowly blinked. "Why, Liam? You can like me a lot, but it can't be the same for me?" She shook her head. "You can't have it both ways, Liam. I like you a lot!" she spat out, her face turning beet red. "There I said it and what are you going to do about it?"

Liam was momentarily shocked at her outburst. Under the seemingly ice-queen exterior was a smoldering fire he'd obviously hadn't expected. She'd admitted men rarely listened to her and therefore dismissed whatever she had to say, but apparently today she wasn't willing to accept it.

Despite a marked difference in their looks, there was something about Charity John that reminded him of Maria Martin. His mother was upbeat and always had a quick smile but rub her the wrong way, and her anger would become a scalding fury that had everyone running in the opposite direction to escape her wrath. But the most obvious difference between the Martins and Johns was they were worlds apart when it came to wealth and lifestyles. Yes, they both were ranchers and that was the only thing they had in common.

He grunted. "I suppose there's not much I can do," he conceded. "I can't change how you feel about me."

"You'll never be able to change how I feel about you," Charity said. "You can take me back now."

She didn't ask but had demanded to be taken back. It was obvious that as the boss's daughter she was used to giving orders and having them obeyed without question.

And why not? As a Bronco Heights John she was comfortable, confident and aware of her rightful place in her world. A world that would never include him nor one he had any wish to become a part of.

He preferred working his own land rather than hiring others to do it for him. He also didn't want to spend his days at a private country club sharing drinks or making deals with other ranchers whose sole intent was to hold on to or concoct schemes to increase their land size and net worth by buying up smaller ranches. And he'd learned a lot serving in the military and it was always a rich man's war and a poor man's fight. Wars meant companies securing government contracts for tanks and other military equipment boosting the profits of CEOs and their shareholders.

The Martins were salt-of-the-earth folks who worked hard to continue their legacy from one generation to the next.

He hadn't lied when he admitted to Charity that he liked her. Liked her enough until it was time for her to return to Bronco. Even with her gone, there would be their connection to Dean Valentini. A connection neither were aware of until Dean's funeral, then meeting again twenty-four hours later. It hadn't mattered whether it was fate or magic. He was forced to accept that something beyond their control had brought them together.

As much as he tried to deny it, Liam felt something with Charity he'd never experienced with any other woman. Despite the fact that she was sheltered while he'd seen the dark side of life, it wasn't for the first time that he'd asked himself if they could really make a go of it. There was one thing he knew: he had to stop second-guessing himself when it came to Charity and let everything unfold naturally.

Liam stood up and extended his hand. "Let's go, princess." She placed her hand in his as he eased her effortlessly to stand. He pointed to her boots. "Don't forget your glass slippers," he teased, smiling.

Leaning closer, Charity kissed his jaw. "I'll put them on in the truck."

Waiting until she picked up her boots, Liam scooped up the blanket and the picnic hamper and carried them to the pickup. Charity had talked about magic, and spending the afternoon together with her was indeed magical. The food, setting and the ease with which he was able to talk to her was something Liam wanted to repeat over and over. They shared a smile as he shifted the truck into gear to begin the ride back, hoping they would continue to see each other when and wherever possible.

"You don't have to walk me in," Charity said when Liam pulled up several feet from the Sanchez home.

He gave her a direct stare. "Are you sure?"

"Very sure." She hesitated. "When will we see each other again?"

"How about tomorrow?"

Her smile was dazzling. "I was hoping you would say that. Call or text and let me to let me know what you're planning."

"Do you like Mexican food?"

"Does a cat flick its tail?"

Throwing back his head, Liam laughed, the sound reverberating in the pickup's interior. "I suppose that's a yes."

"Yes, it's a yes."

"We'll go to Castillo's. The restaurant serves some of the best Mexican food around these parts. Is it all right if I pick you up around six?"

"What if I meet you there?"

A beat passed. "Does your brother have a problem with me dating his sister?"

"Why would you say that?" Charity asked, frowning.

"Maybe my coming to pick you up at his in-laws two days in a row would not sit well with him. It's a known fact that brothers can be overly protective of their sisters."

Charity's blue eyes resembled chips of ice when she glared at him. "For your information my brothers have never interfered with whoever I chose to date. Nor will they ever. That's my decision. I want to meet you at the restaurant because I plan to do some shopping before the stores close. Now, do I need your permission for us to meet at Castillo's at the designated time?"

God help him, but Liam admired that confident streak. "You don't need my permission, Charity, to do anything you want. We'll meet there. Six, okay?"

"Six is perfect. I should be done shopping by that time." Leaning to her left, Charity kissed Liam's jaw. "Thank you again for a wonderful afternoon. And don't forget to thank your mother for taking time to make her delicious dishes."

Smiling and nodding, Liam said, "I'll let her know." He watched Charity get out of the pickup unassisted and walk to the Sanchez front door. She opened it and then waved to him before she closed it.

Even though the door had closed, shutting out her image, Liam still could see the curve of her feminine hips in a pair of body-hugging jeans. Charity hadn't been aware of how difficult it had been for him to keep his hands off her all afternoon. He barely kissed her, when he'd wanted to devour her mouth; it'd taken herculean restraint for him not to deepen the kiss and then strip her naked and make love to her under the heavens.

He'd admitted to going to hell and back, and only now he'd discovered being with Charity filled him with a sense of peace that he hadn't known was missing in his life. If he was good for her, then it went double for him.

Liam walked into the kitchen, carrying the picnic hamper, his eyebrows lifting slightly when he saw his father embracing his mother, one hand cradling her hips. Jack was wearing a suit, and Liam knew he'd just returned to Tenacity from a business trip. He cleared his voice to get their attention, smiling when they jumped apart as if caught doing something they weren't supposed to do.

"Don't mind me. I just came to bring the hamper back."

Jack met Liam's eyes over his wife's head. "How are you feeling?"

"Good."

Jack released his wife. "Just good?"

"Yes, Dad. I'm good." He set the hamper on a stool at the breakfast island and began emptying it.

"That's where we disagree, son. I think you're doing too much. You just got out of the hospital, and you've been overdoing it."

"Grooming horses and mucking the stables is not what I'd call overdoing it," Liam argued as he scraped, rinsed and stacked everything in the dishwasher.

Jack crossed his arms over the front of a crisp pale blue shirt he'd paired with gray suit trousers. "Enzo told me you had a problem picking up a fifty-pound bag of horse feed. Have you forgotten that you had broken one shoulder and dislocated the other?"

"Enzo is a snitch," Liam said under his breath. "And as a member of this family I need to pull my own weight to keep the ranch running."

"He's not a snitch, Liam. He's doing what I've taught all my sons to do. And that is to look out for one another. The ranch survived when you weren't here, and it will survive while you're still here. Starting tomorrow I don't want to see your ass working anywhere on the Double M until after the Fourth of July holiday celebrations. Do I make myself clear, Sergeant Martin?"

Liam glared at his father. "So now we're pulling rank?"

"You better believe it," Jack said angrily.

"We're not in the army, Dad." He recalled whenever Jack would come home on leave, initially he wasn't Dad but Captain Martin. It would take several days for him to shed his military persona and stop barking orders and become the father he and his brothers not only looked up to but also worshipped.

"True, but I'm still the head honcho on the Double M. And I'm telling you—"

"Telling or ordering me?" Liam interrupted.

"Liam, Jack, please!" Maria pleaded, her voice breaking with emotion as she struggled not to cry. "I don't need you fighting with each other. Liam, please listen to your father. He's right about it being too soon for you to start doing chores. You've gone through a lot, and it's going to take time for your body to heal completely. You spent six months in two different hospitals, so not doing anything strenuous for a month should go by quickly. Think of it as a vacation where you can spend time with that girl you've been seeing."

"What girl?" asked Jack, his expression mirroring confusion.

Maria grinned like a Chesire cat. "Our youngest son has been dating a girl from Bronco."

Jack slowly blinked. "For real?"

"Sí, es verdad."

Liam felt as if his family was conspiring against him. Enzo had told their father about his inability to easily pick up a bag of feed, his father was treating him like he was helpless and his mother was no doubt making plans for his wedding. Charity was the only who hadn't attempted to pressure him to do what she wanted.

When he'd asked her to go out with him it was because he'd believed she could possibly help him move forward, and she hadn't hesitated. Liam had come to enjoy every moment with Charity. Perhaps his father giving him a month off from doing chores on the ranch was a blessing in disguise because now he could spend more time with her before she went back to Bronco.

"Okay, Dad. You win. I'll give up doing chores until next month."

Jack gave him an incredulous stare. "So, you're giving up that easily?"

"With you and Mami tag teaming me, I know when to throw in the towel." Liam winked at his mother. "I'm going home to take care of my dog."

"You can bring him around whenever you want," Maria said.

"I thought you didn't like animals in your house."

"I like Harley because he's quiet and he doesn't make a mess."

Liam wanted to tell his mother Harley was only quiet when he was with him. Whenever he was around the other dogs the chasing, barking, nipping and occasional snarling escalated to ear-shattering decibels. It was on the Double M that Harley was free to run and explore his new environment while still retaining the instincts of a military dog.

"I'll bring him tomorrow when I come for breakfast."

Jack dropped an arm over Liam's shoulders. "I'll walk with you to your truck. I need your advice about something."

Liam knew instinctively whatever his father wanted to discuss with him Jack hadn't wanted his wife to overhear. "Okay."

Waiting until they were standing next to the pickup, Jack huffed. "Thank you."

"For what, Dad?"

"For not putting me on the spot where I'd be forced to take sides."

Liam shook his head. This was a Jack Martin he wasn't

familiar with. His father had always been a straight-shooter, saying exactly what was on his mind. “Dad, why are you talking in riddles?”

Jack gave him a direct stare. “When I ordered you not to do any work on the ranch I could see by your expression that we were about to get into it.”

Crossing his arms over his chest, Liam met the older man’s eyes. He’d always looked up to his father who loved and supported his wife and children while serving and protecting his country as an army officer. And over the years his respect never wavered even when Jack had been away from home for long periods of time.

“That’s where you’re wrong, Dad. I’m sure you’re familiar with the military warning ‘it’s not the time.’ It wasn’t the time to get into it with you because Mami looked as if she was about to start crying.”

Jack smothered a curse when he ran a hand over his face. “And she did enough crying to fill a river when we first got the call that you’d been injured. There were times when she cried so much, she had to put ice packs on her swollen eyes to go out in public. Whenever someone mentioned her eyes, she’d lie and say she was suffering from allergies.”

“I don’t envy you, Dad. I’d rather face a court-martial tribunal than deal with a crying woman.”

“Same here, son,” Jack agreed. “It was your mother who wanted me to talk to you about doing work on the ranch after Enzo hinted you were overdoing it. I don’t think he meant any harm, but your mama took it to another level and got in my face that I had to say something to you.”

Smiling, Liam asked, “How close did she get?”

Jack placed his hand against his nose. “This close.”

“Were you scared?” he teased.

“Hell yeah, I was scared. I never told anyone, but there

was a time when your mother threatened to divorce me if I didn't resign my commission. She didn't want her sons to grow up with a part-time father."

Now Liam was confused. "I thought you told me that she was all in with you becoming a soldier."

"She was when we were dating in high school and college. She'd accepted being a military spouse when she had Enzo and Marco. She was living on the ranch, her widowed mother had come to live with us, and my uncles and cousins were running the Double M. Then something changed once you came along. She'd begun complaining that she wanted to go back to teaching, and she wanted her sons to see their father every day and not only when he was granted leave." Jack paused. "I thought she was overwhelmed raising three boys and suggested she leave you guys with her mother and I'd take her on a second honeymoon."

"Did she agree?"

Jack slowly shook his head. "No. What she did was give me an ultimatum—leave the army or she was going to serve me with divorce papers."

"What did you do?"

"I didn't want to lose my wife and kids. We talked about our options, then agreed I would serve for ten years, then as a reservist."

"What if she hadn't agreed, Dad?"

"I would've put in my discharge papers that very day. Even though I loved the military, and I still do, my wife and children were more important to me than anything else in the world. I'm hoping you and your brothers will never be faced with having to choose between love and something you have the ability to control."

"Dad, why are you telling me this now?"

"Because you're at a crossroads in your life, Liam. You

weren't ready to give up the military, yet something beyond your control forced you out. You've been given a second chance because you survived. I know you've tried to hide it, but I know you're suffering from PTSD."

Liam forced a smile. "It's not that bad. The nightmares come and go," he admitted, not wishing to lie to his father.

"Have you discussed them with anyone?"

"I had a few sessions with a psychiatrist at the VA hospital."

"How did that turn out?" Jack questioned.

"They were okay. I know it's going to take a while before I stop reliving what I've gone through. In other words, I'm going to deal with it one day at a time."

"You know I'm always here for you, son."

"I know that, Dad." Liam peered around his father's shoulder to see his mother standing on the porch. "It's time you go back into the house because Mami is watching and wondering what's going on between us."

Jack made a sucking sound with his tongue and teeth. "The older she gets the more she hovers over everyone."

"That's because she loves us." Liam gave his father a hug. "Now, go inside and do what you were planning to with her before I interrupted you."

"What I was planning to do with my wife is something you should think about doing with that girl you're seeing."

"Bye, Dad."

Liam reached for the boots he'd left behind the front seats, slipped into them, then got into the pickup and drove away. What Jack had suggested he do with Charity was a nonstarter. She was only going to be in Tenacity for a couple of weeks, and once she returned to Bronco, Liam doubted they would resume their friendship. And there was still the nagging thought that if she did decide to stay in Tenacity whether he could really have a chance of them being together.

Friends?

Yes.

Friends with benefits?

No!

Chapter Seven

Enzo walked into the kitchen and claimed a seat next to Liam. "What's up with a dog in the house?"

Maria pointed a spatula at her eldest son. "That's not your concern. I asked Liam to bring Harley."

"What makes Harley so special from the other dogs on the ranch?" Enzo questioned.

"The difference is Harley has been trained, while those other sooners would rather feed than fight. The last time you brought one here he would stand in the middle of the kitchen looking for me to drop something on the floor so he could grab it."

"Damn, Mami, why did you have to call our dogs sooners?" Marco grumbled.

"It's been a while since I've heard a dog referred to as a sooner," Jack chuckled.

"Because that's what they are. Liam, do you still like your eggs scrambled?" Maria asked.

"Yes, ma'am." Picking up a coffee mug, he took a sip, then shared a glance with his father.

Enzo filled his mug from the coffee carafe on a trivet. "Even though our dogs are mixed breeds, they still have herding instincts."

Liam smiled at Maria when she set a plate of fluffy

scrambled eggs with sausage patties and fluffy biscuits on the table in front of him. "No one is throwing shade on your pets, big brothers. And you have to admit Harley is getting along well with the three dogs."

Marco pushed back his chair. "Mami, why don't you sit down and eat? I'll finish making breakfast." Four sets of eyes suddenly turned to him. "Why is everyone staring at me?"

Maria sat next to her husband. "If you're practicing cooking, then maybe I'll be claiming a daughter-in-law soon?"

A rush of color further darkened Marco's sun-browned complexion. "That's something you should be asking Liam."

"What about Liam?" Enzo asked Marco.

"The word around Tenacity is that our brother was seen at the Social Club with a young, drop-dead-gorgeous blonde who couldn't take her baby-blue eyes off him."

Jack gave each of his sons a death stare. "Did you forget that you were raised never to kiss and tell? What goes on between Liam and his girlfriend is not a topic for discussion, no more than it's about the women who spend nights in your cabins. Y'all are grown-ass men, so respect one another's private lives."

The three brothers shared smiles, then executed snappy salutes. "Aye, aye, Captain," all chorused in unison.

A hint of a smile lifted the corners of Jack's mouth. "Y'all are lucky you didn't serve under me, because I would've busted every one of you wannabe comedians down to privates."

Maria rested a hand on her husband's arm. "They're just messing with you, Jack. They know you were never in the navy."

Liam, Enzo and Marco exchanged fist bumps. They'd

reverted to boyhood when they would play jokes on their father. Most times he took their teasing in stride, but they were careful not to cross the line to challenge his position as an authority figure. As he matured, Liam realized if he ever were to marry and have children, he'd had the best example of a role model as a husband and father in Jack Martin.

Jack dropped a kiss onto Maria's hair. "I know. I play along to make them think they're getting one over on me. Now that I've cleared my consulting schedule for the rest of the month, if the weather holds, I'm up to cooking out several times a week. What say you, dudes?"

"I'm all in for a fish fry," Enzo volunteered.

"Of course you would be," Marco drawled. "Everyone knows you're the family pescatarian."

Enzo appeared to ignore Marco's jibe when he said, "Y'all don't have to worry about fish, because I caught and froze enough trout and bass to last throughout the summer. And I still have quite a few bags of frozen shrimp, lump crab, lobster tails and calamari."

Liam noticed everyone staring at him. "Okay. I'll grill the steaks."

Jack turned to Maria. "Do we have any steaks left in the freezer chest?"

"The last time I looked we had a couple. I'll call Mrs. Chen at Tenacity Grocery and order enough ribeye, porterhouse and skirt steaks to last for a couple of weekends."

Talking about cooking and eating out with his family conjured up fond memories for Liam. It was a tradition that had always made him feel as if he'd truly come home. He thought about Charity, wondering what rituals or traditions the Johns had established. He finished eating, and when breakfast was over, he stayed to help his mother clean up the kitchen while his father and brothers left to begin working around the ranch.

Liam stacked the last plate in the dishwasher and closed the door. Now that he was forbidden to do chores, he'd planned to go home, put up several loads of laundry and give his cabin a thorough cleaning. "Do you want me to go into town with you when you pick up the steaks?" he asked Maria.

"Thanks for asking, but no. I'll call in the order and have them drop it off here at the ranch. I'll be charged a fee for delivery, but I don't care because I can stay at home watching my telenovelas."

Liam gave her a look mirroring disbelief. "You're still watching those Spanish-language soap operas? I thought you gave them up years ago."

"I stopped once I resumed teaching, but now that I'm retired, I can watch them while I'm cooking or doing housework. What I truly miss is watching them with my mother. I would laugh when she'd start cursing at the television in Spanish because she didn't like a particular character."

Liam also missed his *abuela* who'd insisted her grandsons learn Spanish. He hugged his mother. "I'll see you later."

"You can pick up Harley later."

"What?"

"Leave him here with me so we can become better acquainted. I know you don't feed him until late afternoon, so I'll just put some water out for him."

"Are you attempting to lure my dog away from me?"

"No. If I'd known he was this calm when the army decided to ship him back to the States, I would have taken him in. When I first heard he was a military dog, I'd assumed he would be high-strung and always in attack mode."

Liam didn't tell his mother Harley would attack if given the command. "Once Harley becomes familiar with you, he's quite relaxed."

"We'll find out once you leave."

Walking to where Harley was stretched out in an alcove, Liam knelt, put his arms around the dog's neck and whispered for him to stay. Harley lowered his head and rested his muzzle on his front paws. Like his human partner, the MWD—military working dog—would live out the rest his life as a civilian on the Double M.

"Excuse me, but am I boring you?"

Charity blinked as if coming out of a trance when she registered her sister-in-law's voice. "I'm sorry, Marisa. My mind was someplace else." She'd accompanied Marisa to the ranch where she and Dawson would eventually take up residence once most of the construction was completed.

"Someplace else, or should I say with someone else?"

"What are you trying to say?"

"When I asked you if you wanted to see your guest suite you said you did. But now that we're here you're acting as if your head is in the clouds."

Charity realized Marisa had every right to chastise her. She'd been moping around all morning because she had a lot on her mind.

"Do those things you're thinking about have anything to do with Liam Martin? That maybe you're in love with him?"

Charity stared at Marisa as if she'd taken leave of her senses. "What did you say?"

"I didn't speak Spanish, so you know exactly what I asked, Miss Charity John. A language, by the way, you should learn now that you are in involved with Liam. His mother's family were originally from Mexico."

Charity couldn't believe what she was hearing. Marisa had mentioned her being in love with Liam and learning to speak Spanish in one breath. "No, I am not in love with Liam," she said, enunciating each word. "And I'm not involved with him. We're friends who happen to enjoy each other's company."

"Friends who decide to date the day they're introduced to each other?" Marisa questioned.

"What are you implying, Marisa?"

"That there's something going on between you and Liam you don't want to acknowledge or admit. And apparently, it's bothering you because whenever I speak to you it's as if you're daydreaming."

"I have been thinking about a lot of things," Charity repeated. "And not all of it is about Liam."

"Do you feel comfortable talking about it?"

She met large dark brown eyes, recognizing why her brother had hit the jackpot when he'd fallen in love with and married Marisa Sanchez. She was beautiful, talented, generous and selfless. Marisa had given her the confidence she needed to acknowledge that she was a gifted singer, and she was also keenly aware when Charity attempted to conceal her troubled thoughts behind a too bright smile.

"I don't know what it is, but I feel as if I'm living my life on a carousel, going around and around without stopping or slowing down. I can't get off or even attempt to catch the brass ring. These past few months I've been shuttling between Tenacity and Bronco, in a pattern that's not offering me anything beyond visiting my family. What I'm trying to say is I feel as if my life is on hold, Marisa. Yes,

I'm responsible for the Double J's digital footprint, yet I need something more."

"Do you feel that more whenever you're with Liam?"

"What surprises me is yes. What I like most is talking with him. I can say exactly what is on my mind and not have him judge me or call me silly as some men have done in the past. There is something about him that is so zen that what I feel must be similar to when someone takes a sedative to relax them completely. It's not only his voice but the vibe he projects. And he appears so worldly despite our being only two years apart."

"You have to remember that he was in the military and stationed in different countries around the world and he has seen and experienced a lot. That can mature a person real fast."

Charity nodded. "You're right. He'd mentioned living in the Middle East and was drawn to the culture."

"What else is there about Liam you like?"

"I like him the way a woman likes a man." *Where the heck did that come from? I was about to say I like Liam as a friend. But as a woman likes a man is something else entirely different.* Charity closed her eyes, hoping Marisa didn't notice her faux pas.

Marisa giggled. "And there's no doubt he likes you the way a man likes a woman if he keeps asking you out."

"That's because we enjoy each other's company."

"No, Charity. It's a lot more than that. I saw the way Liam was staring at you during the dig, and it wasn't because he was curious."

"So, now you're a mind reader?" Charity teased.

"No. I'm willing to bet that I've had a lot more experience with men than you have, so I know in an instant when a man is interested in a woman. That included your brother, who when we met was afflicted with the classic love-at-first-sight syndrome. Liam Martin is just as enthralled with you as you are with him."

Charity's eyelids fluttered as a warning voice whispered in her head. Marisa had just diagnosed what was ailing her. She'd tried convincing herself Liam was a friend who'd related to her as an equal rather than some pampered young woman used to getting whatever she wanted. Dating him in Tenacity had opened up a different world from the one she'd experienced in Bronco.

She could see whoever she wanted without Mimi questioning her about her date's pedigree or, even worse, paying a private investigator to do a background check to discover if there were any skeletons in his closet that could possibly damage the Johns' social standing in Bronco Heights.

She raised her eyes to Marisa. "I'm not going to lie and say I don't like him."

"I'm not asking you to lie, Charity. All you have to say is that there's a possibility that Liam Martin may be..."

"May be what?" Charity asked when Marisa didn't finish what she intended to say.

"That he may be the one who can make you happy. The one man who will allow you to live your life on your own terms and not those of Mimi and Randall John. You should know that Dawson told me about the edict your father made. That whichever one of his four children married first in an opulent wedding befitting the Johns' social standing would inherit the largest share of the Double J Ranch."

Charity averted her face, hoping Marisa wouldn't see the flush of embarrassment spreading over her features when she recalled what she'd believed was the most hair-brained, asinine and ludicrous scheme to have ever come out of Randall John's mouth. Back then, Charity wanted to believe she was exempt from the marriage pact, because she was only twenty, so the focus had been on her brothers.

"Those were crazy times, and I'm glad I wasn't brought into it," Charity admitted. "Jameson married Vanessa, Maddox married Adeline Longsworth from the Lazy L Ranch and you married Dawson, who is setting up his own ranch here in Tenacity."

"That only leaves you, Charity. Not only does your mama want to be a mother of the bride, but she also wants you to have an over-the-top wedding."

Charity shook her head. "My mother can forget it because I want something small and intimate like Jameson and Vanessa's wedding. I don't need a fabulous gown which took thousands of hours to make or a huge wedding party." She shuddered. "I'm certain my mother would order enough flowers to make the Double J resemble a botanical garden. And of course, there would be ice sculptures, several live bands and a six-tiered wedding cake." She paused. "I don't know why we're talking about weddings when I'm not even engaged."

"Do you want to be engaged?" Marisa asked her.

Charity smiled. "Can you please let me fall in love first before you talk about me becoming engaged?"

Marisa held up both hands. "No more talk about weddings or engagements. Until Liam puts a ring on your finger," she whispered under her breath.

"I heard that, Marisa Sanchez-John."

"I'm sorry. I was just thinking out loud."

Charity didn't know if it was wishful thinking on Marisa's part or if she actually wanted to believe what her sister-in-law had blurted out. She liked Liam. A lot. However, she had to ask herself if he was someone she could imagine marrying and spending the rest of her life with.

What Charity didn't want was a list of things she wanted and expected from a man similar to those her parents had created for their children. For Randall and Mimi, wealth and social pedigree topped the criteria for a suitable marriage. The wealthier the better, and belonging to the Association was definitely a plus.

The man she was currently dating wasn't wealthy, didn't own a sprawling ranch in Bronco Heights, and the Martins were not members of a private club. None of that mattered to Charity. She would continue to date Liam until their relationship reached that inevitable point where either they would agree to breakup or stay together. Staying together would result in her moving from Bronco to Tenacity. Charity did not see it as a dealbreaker because Dawson left the Double J to relocate and start up his own ranch in Tenacity.

"You need to mute your thoughts so others can't hear what you're thinking."

Marisa looped her arm through Charity's. "I promise to try and tell them not to be so noisy. I know you told me that you have a date with Liam later tonight, so do you want to see more of the ranch or go back to the house?"

"I'd like to see what they've done to the stables."

Her brother had invested a small fortune purchasing the abandoned ranch to repair all the structures, while updating and expanding the main house. Growing up and working on the Double J had given him the wherewithal to run his own ranch. Charity also wasn't a novice to ranch life. Even when she'd left Bronco to attend college, she'd counted down the days till it came time for her to return home. Bronco was always home…but the more time she'd begun spending in Tenacity, the more it felt like home, too.

Liam stood outside Castillo's, waiting for Charity. He'd arrived early, hoping she hadn't gotten there before him.

He didn't have to wait long when he spied her crossing the street to meet him. Her movements were as graceful as a dancer's, and Liam wasn't able to pull his gaze away from the slim-cut jeans she'd paired with a white poet's blouse and low-heeled boots. She'd styled her hair in a mass of tiny golden curls framing her face and tumbling over her shoulders.

He smiled. Charity was a chameleon. Each time he saw her she looked different. A smile crossed her delicate features when she stopped in front of him. Dipping his head, he pressed a kiss to her cheek, inhaling the sensual scent of perfume on her neck, a light floral fragrance matching her sunny personality.

"Did you get all of your shopping done?"

Charity leaned into him, her chest barely touching his, smiling. "Not really. I'd planned to visit several stores, but once I walked into the consignment shop, Nothin' New, I ended up spending all my time there."

"Were you browsing or buying?"

"I managed to do both. I left my purchases in my vehicle."

Liam opened the door to Castillo's, holding it while Charity walked in, then followed her. Although Tenacity claimed a number of restaurants and places to eat, Castillo's had become one of his favorites because of their reputation for serving authentic Mexican food. And despite being housed in a narrow storefront with two rows of wooden booths and a bar in the back, it was dark enough to provide for a modicum of intimacy. Mouthwatering aromas wafted from the restaurant's kitchen where Pablo and Yolanda Castillo had spent at least thirty years serving up delicious dishes to locals and visitors alike.

"This place is really cozy," Charity whispered. She sniffed the air. "And something smells good."

Resting a hand at the small of her back, Liam led her over to an empty wooden booth, glad he'd suggested coming at six because the restaurant was nearly filled to capacity. He seated Charity, then rounded the table to sit opposite her. The soft, golden glow from a gaslight-inspired hanging pendant illuminated her delicate features.

"I may sound biased, but everything that comes out of Castillo's kitchen is delicious."

"You can say that again," said a deep voice, speaking Spanish.

Liam's head popped up when he recognized the owners' youngest son, who now helped out in the kitchen. Rising to stand, he and Enrique Castillo exchanged handshakes and rough hugs. "How have you been?" he asked the young man everyone called Ricky, replying in the same language.

"That's what I should be asking you, Liam. I'd heard you were in an accident and had to leave the military. So, how the hell are you?"

"I'm good, Ricky." That had become his pat answer for everyone who inquired about his health.

Enrique took a quick glance at Charity. "Aren't you going to introduce me to your girlfriend?" he asked in rapid Spanish.

Liam knew introducing Charity John as his girlfriend would spread like wildfire throughout Tenacity. There already was talk about them being seen together at the Social Club when he'd announced he'd been waiting for his date.

He smiled at her. "Charity, this is Enrique Castillo, who has continued his family's reputation of serving some of the best Mexican-inspired dishes in the county. Ricky, Charity John."

Charity extended her hand, smiling. "It's a pleasure to meet you."

Enquire took her hand and dropped a kiss onto the back of it. "It is truly my honor to meet you," he crooned, his sonorous voice lowering to an even deeper octave.

Liam glared at Enrique as if he'd suddenly lost his mind. He didn't want to believe the man was openly flirting with his girlfriend. "That's enough handholding," he spat out in Spanish.

"*¿Celoso?*" Enrique questioned, grinning.

"*¡No. Posesivo!*" Liam countered angrily.

The cook released Charity's hand, then held up both of his. "No harm done. I just needed to know where you were coming from." He winked at Charity. "You better hold on to his man because he will also protect you," he told her, switching back to English. "I have to get back to the kitchen to help Mom and Pop because tonight we have a full house. Someone will be with you to take your orders. Good seeing you again, Liam. And please don't be a stranger."

Liam nodded, forcing a smile. "I promise I won't."

His initial annoyance with Enrique vanished once he realized the cook wasn't really flirting with Charity. When he'd asked Liam if he was jealous, it was something he did not want to admit, because then he would have to reexamine his emotions and acknowledge what he felt for her went beyond friendship.

Liam had been very, very careful not to cross the line to wordlessly demonstrate to Charity that each and every time they were together it had become more and more difficult for him not to kiss her, because he knew if he did, he wouldn't stop until he'd ask to make love to her. He'd resorted to taking ice-cold showers and staying up late watching mindless television. The night before he was so exhausted that he'd fallen asleep on the living room sofa and only woke when Harley attempted to climb up next to him. That was when he'd asked himself if he could continue to see Charity every day and remain friends; the voice in his head said yes because each day brought her closer to when she would leave Tenacity to return home to Bronco.

Charity stared at Liam when he retook his seat. "How often do you speak Spanish?" Although she hadn't understood a word he'd exchanged with the man he called Ricky, something told her they were discussing her.

"Not that often. I'll occasionally speak it with my mother, but only to keep fluent."

"What did he say about me?"

"He who?"

Charity leaned over the table. "Don't play obtuse, Liam. What did Ricky say to you about me?" she asked between clenched teeth.

Liam slowly blinked, then lowered his eyes. "He asked if I was jealous because he was holding your hand much too long to be polite."

Charity sat back. "And what did you tell him?" Liam met her eyes, and she knew the answer even before he spoke. There was no doubt that he was jealous.

"I told him I wasn't jealous but possessive, and that means I don't want to share you with another man. I hope that answers your question."

There was a barely perceptible nod of her head as she stared over his shoulder. "Yes and no."

"Why the no, Charity?"

"Will I have to share you with another woman?"

He smiled, and the warmth of the gesture lit up his entire handsome face. "Never."

Buoyed with this pronouncement, a powerful sense of relief flowed through Charity. She had no idea where her relationship with Liam Martin would lead, yet in that instant she vowed to make their every second, minute, hour and day together memorable enough for her hold on to for a very long time.

Smiling, she reached for a plastic-covered menu and scanned the selections. "Because this is my first time coming here, I'm going to let you order for me."

Liam barely glanced at the menu. "Can you handle spicy foods?"

"I'm okay if it's not too, too spicy." She didn't want to eat something so hot, then end up with blisters on her tongue.

"I'll make certain to tell our server to tone down the spice level. Is it all right if we begin with soup and appetizers before ordering entrées?"

"Yes, Liam. And please place our orders before my stomach starts making noises and embarrasses us." Charity had purposefully skipped lunch because she knew she going to have dinner with Liam.

As if on cue, a server approached their table, and Liam ordered what he wanted in fluent Spanish. Hearing him speak the language reminded Charity of Marisa's suggestion she should learn Spanish now that she was involved with Liam. Although she'd denied being involved with him, she'd come to realize it wasn't as much an involvement but a strange and magical connection that didn't appear to be real. It was as if she was a character in a paranormal novel who was living in an alternative universe.

Charity had to remind herself that she wasn't a four-year-old little girl whose mother read her fairytales about princes and princesses falling in love and living happily-ever-after. She was now a twenty-four-year-old woman who'd had a string of meaningless dates beginning in high school and throughout college only to realize she'd been wasting her time with men who either bored her to tears or sought something from her once they discovered she was a ranch heiress.

Liam Martin was different from all the other men in her past, and it wasn't until Marisa introduced them at the dinosaur dig that Charity realized Liam was the man she hadn't known she'd been searching for. Marisa had asked if she was in love with Liam and she'd half lied to her sister-in-law.

She wasn't in love with Liam.

But she was falling in love with him.

Chapter Eight

Charity took a sip of sangria and closed her eyes. "Wow! This is delicious."

"Beautiful company, delicious food and good drinks," Liam drawled. "That's what I call a trifecta."

She wanted to tell Liam that he was a trifecta of everything she wanted in a man, because with him she felt as if they were on equal footing. He treated her like an adult and not someone who needed talking down to. It hadn't mattered if she'd dated men closer to her age or even older, they invariably related to her as if what she'd say didn't matter.

There were times, and usually not more than a nanosecond whenever she met Liam's eyes, that Charity believed he knew what she was thinking. He was the first man she'd met where she'd felt so strongly a connection that if he'd asked, she would've been willing to sleep with him this early in a relationship. The mere thought had shaken her to her core, because she'd never felt that way before. She didn't know what there was about Liam where her thoughts veered in a direction she deemed reckless.

She'd been accused of being fickle but never reckless. Not even in her so-called rebellious adolescence. She'd occasionally broken curfew, indulged in underage drinking, but opted out when her girlfriends formed a pact to give up their virginity. Then she met Nick, who was rich enough to gain her parents' approval, but at twenty she hadn't been ready to tie the knot, much to Mimi John's disappointment. Even then, Charity wasn't certain whether she'd wanted to spend the rest of her life with Nick or on the Double J.

Some twentysomethings were faced with having to move back home to live with their parents after graduating college because they had to repay student loans or didn't earn enough for them to live on their own. It was different for Charity; she had her own suite of rooms in the main house at the Double J. And despite all the amenities of living at home, being paid a generous salary for overseeing the ranch's digital footprint, she was unable to control her destiny. It didn't take the intelligence quotient of an astrophysicist for her to realize that wasn't possible until she left the ranch.

Charity picked up a knife and fork, cut a *sope*, a small round fried corn cake topped with beans, cheese, salsa and pork carnitas, in half and took a forkful, her eyes widening in surprise. When Liam had suggested having soup and appetizers before ordering entrées, she never could've imagined dishes that tasted so amazing. She was more than familiar with tacos, fajitas, grilled Mexican street corn and guacamole; however, sampling the *albondigas* soup, *sopes* and flautas, crispy rolled tortillas filled with chicken and beef and served with guacamole and pico de gallo, was something she wanted to experience over and over.

"Hanging out with you has spoiled me," she said after swallowing a mouthful of deliciousness.

"How so?" Liam asked.

"I want to share meals like this with you every night of the week."

His dark eyes came up as if to study her face, and Charity was suddenly aware of what she'd said. Had he believed she was hinting about their possibly living together?

There was complete silence. It grew more uncomfortable for Charity until Liam smiled. "You want to eat at Castillo's every night?"

Charity realized she'd been caught up in her own emotions. Liam hadn't read more into her suggestion than warranted. "I know it sounds a little crazy, but I'm ready to sample everything on the menu. I've had Mexican food before, but never anything like this."

"It's because most restaurants cater to what has become commercial Mexican dishes like tacos, fajitas, burritos and enchiladas. My *abuela* used to make *tetelas*, which is a traditional *antojito*, or street food, from Oaxaca."

Charity took another sip of sangria. "How are they made?"

"They are little masa pockets shaped like triangles and filled with refried beans and Oaxacan cheese, then cooked on a flat griddle called a comal. The refried beans are made from black beans, jalapeños, onion and garlic. They can be served as a snack, appetizer for lunch and dinner."

"I love refried beans. Will you make some for me if we have another picnic?"

Liam chuckled. "Damn, woman. No one would ever accuse you of being subtle."

Charity smiled. "There's no need to beat around the bush when you want something."

"And do you always get what you want?"

Her smile vanished quickly. Had Liam believed because she was a John all of her wishes were granted? If that were true, then she would be like her brothers. She could fall in love and marry whoever she wanted and not someone her who parents had selected for her.

"No, Liam. I don't always get what I want because sometimes it isn't what I need."

Charity closed her eyes for several seconds as she struggled not to lose her temper. "Need isn't always about material things," she stated in a low controlled voice. "A baby has no need for money because all he or she needs is to be fed, changed and cradled to feel a mother's or father's love."

He nodded. "You're right. I'm sorry I misspoke."

"Apology accepted."

Liam realized he'd put his boot in his mouth when he'd accused Charity of being a spoiled little rich girl who was able to get anything and everything she wanted from her parents. Yes, she was born into wealth, but he also wondered if she would be willing to give up her pampered lifestyle to become the wife of someone who didn't have the resources to hire staff to work their ranch and was forced to rely on family members to keep it viable, much like the majority of ranches in Tenacity. Her wealth had protected her against the harsher realities of life and more importantly he didn't want to burst that bubble by exposing her to PTSD.

He pointed to the empty platter. "Do you want more appetizers?"

An attractive blush darkened Charity's complexion. "Yes. I'd like a few more beef and chicken flautas. After that then we can order entrées."

Liam turned his head to conceal a smirk. It had been a while since he'd dated a woman who hadn't monitored everything she ate. He remembered dating one who blotted the olive oil off a slice of pizza because she claimed she was on a strict diet to consume less than a thousand calories a day in order not to gain weight. Liam didn't begrudge her dietary limitations because they were personal, but when she tended to tell him what he should or shouldn't eat, that was when he'd severed all contact with her.

Beckoning to their server, he told the woman what he wanted, thanked her, then returned his attention to Charity. "Tell me about Bronco."

"What do you want to know?"

"Everything."

Leaning back in the booth Charity met his eyes. "The Heights is where some of the wealthiest families in the state live, while the Valley is more blue collar and middle class."

"Do Valley folks ever mingle with those in the Heights?"

Charity went still. "Yes. They are able to shop in the same stores if they can afford it. The Heights are more upscale. Beaumont and Rossi's Fine Jewels, BH Couture, and DJ's Deluxe are among the few."

Liam chuckled. "The adjectives attached to these establishments like *fine*, *couture* and *deluxe* mean they are hoity-toity."

"Not all establishments can be known by one name like Tiffany's, Cartier, Apple or Nike—therefore the adjectives."

"True," he agreed. "If you decided to leave the Double J, but didn't want to move away from Bronco, where would you live?"

"I'd probably move into BH247. It's an apartment complex in Bronco Heights that's popular with a lot of single professionals because of its amenities and the magnificent views of the mountains."

Charity had given Liam an answer he would've predicted, that she would make a lateral move when leaving the opulence of the Double J to move into an upscale apartment building in tony Bronco Heights. However, he was surprised that she'd admitted shopping at Nothing' New,

Tenacity's consignment shop. "Where do the folks in the Valley work?"

"There are employment opportunities in the Heights, so it's convenient for them to work there. But people in the Valley own a number of mom-and-pop shops like here in Tenacity. Doug's is a popular hole-in-the-wall bar. Sadie's Holiday House is a gift shop that celebrates Christmas all year long."

"You're kidding?"

Charity shook her head. "No. The shops smells of pine trees and cinnamon, and cheerful holiday music is played twelve months a year. The decorations would challenge Fifth Avenue department stores windows during the Christmas season. Folks claim it's like Hansel and Gretel's house on steroids. It's one of my favorite places to shop other than Cimarron Rose. The boutique opened a couple of years ago, and it's where I buy all of my bohemian-cowgirl-chic outfits. The dress I wore when I met you at the Social Club and this blouse came from her boutique."

"And you always look incredible. Did I embarrass you?" Liam questioned when Charity lowered her eyes, unaware of how sensual he found the gesture.

"A little," she admitted.

Now Liam was confused. There was no doubt Charity did not lack for attention from men who pursued her, so why the slight blush that colored her cheeks?

"I didn't mean to embarrass you, Charity, and if you rather I not say anything about your appearance, then I won't."

"It's not that."

"Then, what is it?" he asked.

Charity prayed what she planned to reveal to Liam wouldn't end whatever hope she had to continue to go out with him. “You’re different than any other man I’ve known. I’ve wracked my brain asking myself over and over what it is, and I still haven’t come up with an answer. If you think I’m shameless, then I want you to tell me.”

Liam leaned over the table. “Shameless about what?” he whispered.

“When you kissed me yesterday, I didn’t want you to stop until we made love with each other.”

He slowly pressed his back against the booth. “Do you realize what could’ve happened if we did? I wasn’t carrying protection—”

“And I’m not on birth control,” she said, interrupting him.

Liam shook his head. “And the possibility of me getting you pregnant is not something I take lightly, Charity. We’re not in love with each other, and I’d never pressure you to marry me because you were carrying my child. And besides, I wasn’t raised to become a baby daddy, and I suspect it’s the same with you becoming a baby mama.”

“It is,” she admitted. She hadn’t planned on becoming a mother before marriage; however, if it did happen despite taking precautions, then it was beyond her control.

“At least we both can agree on that. I don’t need your mother screaming at my mother about what her son did to her daughter or your father coming to Tenacity with a shotgun, demanding I marry his little girl. And if your brothers and mine were to tangle in a so-called cage match it would turn into a feud between Bronco and Tenacity families that would last for decades.”

Charity laughed, the sound carrying where other diners turned to glance her way. “Why,” she whispered, “are you being so dramatic?”

“You believe bringing a child into this world isn’t dramatic, Charity? It's amazing and life-changing for couples who create a new life through the most intimate act of lovemaking."

She stared at Liam, complete surprise freezing her features. Charity found herself caught off guard by this unpredictable man she'd believed she was beginning to understand. Suddenly it hit her that Liam would never allow her to get to know him well. There was something in his personality he'd kept guarded, as if he opened up then it would make him vulnerable. Charity didn't know if his brush with death had changed him or if he was the same sensitive man before his injuries.

"I'm willing to bet my mother would be overjoyed knowing she's going to have another grandchild. My brother Maddox and his wife, Adeline, have a little boy they named Matthew."

"You mother has one up on mine because Maria complains constantly that none of her sons are even remotely thinking about making her an *abuela*."

"How old are your brothers?" Charity asked.

"Enzo is thirty and Marco twenty-eight."

"Tell your mother not to worry. All my brothers were close to or in their thirties once they decided to marry."

Liam grunted. "You can try and convince her of that. She won't listen to any of us whenever we say we want to take our time finding that special woman. We're like our father because once we commit, then it's forever."

"How old was your father when he married your mother?"

"Twenty-two. He'd just graduated college and was scheduled to be deployed. My parents were high school sweethearts who got engaged during their junior year in college.

My mother went to Montana State in Billings to become a teacher and my dad enrolled in the ROTC in Southern University. After graduating as a lieutenant, he was assigned to an intelligence communications unit because of his expertise in electronic engineering.

"Mami taught school for a couple of years before becoming pregnant. She was a stay-at-home wife and mother until I came along. Once she decided to return to the classroom her mother came to live with us. It was my grandmother who spoke only Spanish to me and my brothers because she wanted us fluent."

"Your mother didn't speak Spanish to you?"

"Not as often as her mother because she wanted us to grow up bilingual. Unfortunately, Dad never bothered to learn more than a few words, so we would talk about him without him understanding what we were saying."

"Did any of your brothers join the ROTC?"

"No. Marco and Enzo both have business degrees. My plan after graduating high school was to enlist and eventually work as a federal agent in the army's Criminal Investigation Division."

"What about the Double M?" Charity asked.

"What about it?"

"You wouldn't have returned to the Double M?"

"Of course." Reaching across the table, Liam took her hand. "I told you before that ranching is a part of what makes me who I am and all I'll ever be." He paused meeting her eyes. "What about you, Charity?"

Charity stared into large eyes that reminded her of rich dark coffee. "What about me?" she asked, answering his question with one of her own.

"What have you planned for your future?"

Liam had asked her an easy question "Like you, ranching is also a part of who I am. One day I hope to fall in love and marry and raise my children on land that is a part of my family's legacy."

He gave her hand a gentle squeeze. "In other words, you plan to stay in Bronco and marry a rancher."

A mysterious smile parted her lips. Charity couldn't tell Liam that she wanted to fall in love and marry a man like him—someone gentle, kind, calming, and sensitive and with whom she'd feel loved and protected. "Yes. I want to marry a rancher. What about you, Liam? What if you meet a woman who didn't want to become a rancher's wife?"

Liam released her hand. "Then it would be a dealbreaker. We would have to be on the same page from the beginning of our relationship, even if it meant living together to see if it was what she actually wanted."

"What if she decided ranch life wasn't for her?"

"Then, no hard feelings, babe."

"Even if you truly were in love with her?"

"Loving, Charity, is knowing when to let go so the other person can find their true happiness."

"The words sound good, but I'm not sure that's realistic."

"Aren't you too young to be so cynical?"

"I'm not too young to know what I don't want. As the youngest in my family, and the only girl, I've had to live my life according to rules set up by other people."

A half smile crossed Liam's face. "That's life, Charity. Even as adults there are still rules we're expected to follow. But I broke those rules when, as the youngest in my family, it was expected I attend college like my parents and brothers, but then all hell broke loose once I told my mother I intended to enlist in the army rather than go to college. There was an exchange of a lot of harsh words and a few hurt feelings, and once I realized there would be no winner or loser I decided to compromise."

Charity waited until the server set another dish of flautas on the table and walked away before asking Liam, "What did you do?"

"I used my GI Bill education benefit to earn a criminal justice degree."

"You were forced to compromise to please your mother?" Charity watched the familiar mask flit over his features, realizing he was shutting her out again. And whenever she witnessed it, she found it unnerving. "I'm sorry, Liam. I shouldn't have said that."

"There's no need for you to apologize. You said what you meant."

"But I didn't mean for it to come out like it did."

"Charity."

He'd said her name so softly she thought that she'd imagined it. "Yes?"

"Please let it go."

"Okay." He'd asked her to let it go, and she would. However, forgetting what she'd said wasn't going to be so easy.

"You can continue to eat the flautas, but we should order our entrées."

Charity felt a wave of relief once she realized the tense moment had passed. At least it had for her. "I'm not certain whether I'll be able to finish an entire entrée after loading up on soup and appetizers."

"Order one to go, and save it for tomorrow's lunch or dinner," Liam suggested.

"I'll probably have it for breakfast."

Liam gave her an incredulous stare. "You eat dinner for breakfast?"

"Don't look so surprised. Folks do it all the time."

"Do they?"

Resting an elbow on the table, she cupped her chin on the heel of her hand. "I shared an apartment in college with two Southern girls. One was from the Carolina Low-country, and the other one grew up in New Orleans. We would spend the weekend cooking for the entire week, so all we had do was heat up whatever we wanted to eat on a particular day. I can't tell you how many times I had shrimp and grits, gumbo or fried chicken for breakfast."

Liam flashed a wide grin. "That place must have been smelling really good."

Charity scrunched up her nose. "You don't know the half of it."

"How did you decide on what you wanted to cook?"

"We'd sit down and plan a menu, then figure out how much we wanted to spend for groceries. But that depended on what was on sale at the supermarket. My roommate from South Carolina was a finance major, so she was the one who was responsible for budgeting what we'd buy. Living with those girls and learning to budget my money was new for me because my mother always took care of the Double J's household."

"It sounds as if you were able to get two educations for the price of one."

"You're right. I was able to learn invaluable life skills that have allowed me to become an independent adult more than capable of living on my own."

"Is that what you want, Charity? To live on your own?"

More than anything else in the world. I want to be able to get up and go to sleep in my own place where I'm in control of everything. I want to be able to date whoever I choose without my date having to go through an inquisition and reveal who his people are and how much he's worth.

"It's somewhere at the top my wish list," she said.

"It's not as if you don't have options," Liam stated. "You said there are apartments you can rent in Bronco Heights if you choose not to leave your hometown."

"That is definitely something to consider." Charity didn't want to tell Liam that moving from the Double J into an apartment at BH247 wouldn't put enough distance between her and her parents to stop them from monitoring her social life.

"Bronco seems like a nice place to live whether in the Heights or Valley."

"It is," Charity confirmed. "I'd love for you to come with me for dinner at DJ's Deluxe. It some of the finest cuts of meats in the county, an extensive wine list and wonderful craft beers. I'd have to make a reservation in advance, with Saturday nights filling up months in advance."

"You want us to drive over an hour and a half to a restaurant just to eat dinner?"

Charity lowered her arm. "Yes. I can assure you the drive will be more than worth it. If we leave early enough, I'll be able to give you a tour of both Broncos."

Attractive lines fanned out around Liam's eyes when he smiled. "Bronco sounds great. There has to be something in Tenacity's water that lures folks from Bronco to settle here."

"Tenacity happens to be quite charming."

Liam's eyebrows lifted slightly. "I've never heard anyone refer to Tenacity as charming."

"Well, it is to me," Charity insisted. "I'm aware that all towns and cities have their problems, but whenever I come to here to visit my brother and Marisa, I feel something I don't experience in Bronco. I can't quite put my finger on it, though."

"Maybe you'll discover what it is before it's time for you to head back."

She didn't want to think about going back to Bronco. Not now, and not when she was experiencing a sense of ultimate freedom to do and go wherever she wanted. And more importantly, date whoever she wanted.

Back when she was enrolled in college, she'd been financially dependent on her family. Things were different now being on the Double J's payroll. She was paid well for the work she did, and because she didn't have living expenses, she'd been able to invest most of her salary and still have a good sum at her disposal.

She pulled her thoughts up short and looked at him. "I can't believe I've been running off at the mouth making plans when you may have responsibilities on the Double M."

"Right now, I'm on the IL for the month. That's baseball jargon for the injured list."

Charity gasped. "Did you just injure something?"

"No. It's just that I'm taking it easy for the rest of the month—I'm trying not to overdo it."

She placed a hand over her throat. "You had me frightened for a moment."

"Sorry about that. And I don't mind you talking because I like listening to your voice."

Charity lowered her eyes. "Thank you." Liam liked her voice while she liked everything about him, enough to openly admit to him she'd wanted to sleep with him.

Liam got their server's attention and ordered entrées, indicating he wanted one to go. "It's going to take me days to eat all that you ordered for me."

"Not if you share it with Dawson and Marisa."

"Aren't you going to order something for your family?"

"Nope. The Martins are capable of making at least half the dishes on the Castillo's menu."

"Bragging, Liam?"

He winked at her. "No. Just stating the facts."

"Maybe one of these days when I get the chance to come back to Tenacity, I'll ask you to cook for me."

"Okay."

"Really?" she asked, shocked that he'd agreed so quickly.

"Sí, yo prometo concinar para ti."

"I took French in high school and college, so you're going to have to translate what you just said."

"I said I promise to cook for you. And if you planned to spend more than two weeks here, I'd tutor you in Spanish, too."

Charity recalled Marisa telling her to learn the language now that she was involved with Liam, while she'd asked herself if they were actually committed to each other. And the answer had been no. They were friends who'd continue to see each other until it came time for her to return to the Double J.

"Even if I spent a month here, I doubt if I'd be able to learn that much," she told him.

"You'd be surprised how much you'll come to understand. It may take a while before you're fluent, though."

"How long is a while, Liam?"

"At least a year."

"A lot of things can happen in a year. If I decide to move in with Dawson and Marisa, then we can schedule a time when you could tutor me."

"What about your job at the Double J?"

"I can set up a hybrid schedule where I'll spend two or

three days in Bronco and the rest of the week here in Tenacity."

"So, our little town is really growing on you," Liam teased.

It's not the town but one man.

Chapter Nine

Liam walked into the family room and smiled. His mother appeared to be mesmerized as she stared at the television mounted above the fireplace. She was watching one of her favorite telenovelas, and he knew not to interrupt her until there was a commercial break.

He shook his head, wondering why the episodes were filled with over-the-top melodrama depicting passion, outbursts of anger and always an abundance of tears. Liam didn't begrudge his mother her guilty pleasure; she was more than entitled to do whatever made her happy. She didn't know her husband was planning to take her away for a month the following year to tour several islands in the South Pacific, Australia and New Zealand to celebrate their thirty-fifth wedding anniversary. Liam, along with Enzo and Marco, had vowed to keep Jack's plan a secret.

The scene ended with a sobbing actress pleading with her husband who'd seen her kissing another man and swearing she wasn't cheating on him. "Was she really cheating?" he asked his mother.

Maria shook her head. "No. He was her ex who wanted her back, and when he saw her husband walk into the room, he kissed her to make him jealous." She turned to look at

Liam. "Did something happen? Why didn't you join us for breakfast?"

"I don't know what Harley got into after I let him out for his morning run, but he came back smelling as if he'd tangled with a skunk, so I had to wash him twice to get rid of the odor."

"Marco mentioned he saw a couple of baby skunks over near the barn, so that's probably where Harley encountered them. He claims he's going put out some traps and once they're caught, he's going to relocate them somewhere far away from the ranch."

"I just came to tell you that I'm going into town for a haircut. Is there anything you want me to bring back for you?"

"No, thank you. I have everything I need." Maria paused. "Do you plan to eat dinner with the family tonight?"

"Yes. Is there anything else you'd like to know?" Maria asking if he was going to eat with the family was her subtle way of asking if he was going to see Charity.

"Nope. I was just wanted to know if I should put out a plate for you."

Liam gave his mother a *you've not fooling me* look. "You always set the table for Dad and your boys. And when one doesn't show up you just remove the plate."

"I was just asking."

"If you want to know if I plan to see Charity tonight, then the answer is no."

When he left her in the parking lot the night before, he'd kissed her cheek, thanked her for a wonderful evening, then waited for her to drive away before getting into his own vehicle to drive back to the ranch.

Sharing dinner with Charity at Castillo's and her admitting wanting him to make love to her at the picnic was not only unexpected but totally shocking. It was as if she'd read his mind because if he'd had protection there was no doubt both their fantasies would've been fulfilled. He'd also been forthcoming when he told her it was something that could not happen because neither was prepared for an unplanned pregnancy.

Did he want to make love to her?

Yes, he did.

Was he ready to father a child?

No way!

Liam knew he was old-school, because he wanted to fall in love, marry and then start a family. In that order.

He dropped a kiss onto his mom's cheek. "I'll see you later."

Maria waved, then turned to focus on the screen. "Later, *mi amor.*"

Liam chuckled. Everyone was "my love" to his mother. It was most obvious when she would call one son by the other's name, and when corrected, then it would become *mi amor.* His brothers used to tease her saying she was lucky she only had three kids, because any more would've confused her even more. What Liam found astounding was she never forgot the names of any of her students. Whenever they went into town, she would acknowledge each child by name who'd shyly greet Mrs. Martin.

Liam had just slipped behind the wheel of the Ram when he heard a rumble of thunder off in the distance. Within seconds the sky darkened, and he knew rain was imminent. He started the engine and drove away from the ranch, increasing his speed and hoping to make it into town before the skies opened up. He'd just pulled into a parking space when fat drops splattered the windshield. Getting out he sprinted to the building housing the barber shop, along with the post office, and the Social Club located in the basement.

"Well, well, well. Look what the cat drug in."

Liam smiled at the barber who'd been cutting hair longer than he'd been alive. "How's it going, Hank?"

Hank Johnson extended a heavily-veined hand. "That's what I should be asking you, soldier."

Liam pumped Hank's hand. It was apparent the barber wasn't aware of his injuries, and he had no intention of enlightening him. "No more soldiering, Hank. I'm back to ranching."

"Like your father?"

"Yup. You know we Martins can't stay away from the Double M for too long."

"I know what you mean. Ranching is like a woman. You can't live with her, then once you leave you realize you can't live without her." He pointed to an empty chair. "Sit down, son, and you have to let me know how much you want me to cut off."

Liam removed his Stetson and sat, staring at his reflection in the wall of mirrors. "I want it cropped close to my scalp." Whenever he let his hair grow out it tended to curl, then he was forced to put product on it to make it manageable.

"How about a shave?"

Liam rarely let a day go by when he didn't shave; however, it had been a while since he'd had a professional hot-towel shave. He rubbed his jaw. "Okay. Haircut and a shave."

The rain had stopped by the time he walked out of the barbershop an hour later and into the hot, humid air that was a reminder of when he'd gone to Miami with several buddies during a weeklong leave before they were scheduled to be shipped overseas. During the summer months it rained every day around the same time; once it stopped the humidity made it feel as if he'd stepped into a sauna.

Liam checked his cell phone for the time. He had two more hours before he had to return to the ranch for dinner. For some reason he felt like a tourist in his own town when he strolled down streets with stores that had been in business for years and several newer ones. Then he had to remember it had been two years since he'd last come home.

He stopped in front Tiffany in Bloom. Charity had mentioned the owner was engaged to Ellis Corey. Liam was familiar with the Coreys, Black ranchers who owned the Circle C. Ellis's grandmother, Angela Corey, co-owner of Little Cowpokes Daycare Center, had earned the reputation of making the best mac and cheese in the entire state of Montana.

Liam peered into the window, and wondered if Charity would like some flowers. There was only way to find out. He went in and stood off to the side waiting for the owner of the shop who'd just finished wrapping a bouquet of varying shades of yellow flowers in pale blue cellophane for an elderly man. Liam picked up a business card with *Tiffany in Bloom* and the owner's name, Tiffany Brandt, embossed in flowing script on the square of vellum.

He chanced a quick glance at her and knew why Ellis had been taken with her. She was stunning. Tall, slender, with long black hair, her big brown eyes that crinkled when she smiled at something her customer said. Then she laughed, and Liam couldn't help smiling when he heard the infectious sound.

Tiffany finished processing her customer's purchase, thanked him, then turned her attention to Liam once the man exited the shop. “Good afternoon. Is there something I can help you with?”

He glanced around the space with potted plants in colorful hand-painted pots, hanging baskets overflowing with leaves and flowers, and buckets of fresh flowers stored in a refrigerated space behind a wall of glass.

“I’d like buy some flowers for someone.”

“Do you have an idea what type of flowers the person would like?”

“I… I don’t know because I’ve never given her flowers.”

A hint of a smile lifted the corners of Tiffany’s mouth. “You want to give flowers to a woman?” Liam nodded. “How old is the woman?”

Liam stared at Tiffany’s flawless brown complexion. “She’s probably around your age.”

“Thirtyish?”

He shook his head. “She’s more like twenty-four.”

“Oh, I see,” Tiffany said softly. “Tell me something about her.”

Liam had never given a woman flowers before, and now he had to analyze Charity’s personality. “Outwardly, she appears younger than she actually is. There are times when she’s very demure and projects a certain innocence—” He didn’t add boldness. He’d been pleasantly shocked when Charity had mentioned making love.

“I know what you need,” Tiffany said, cutting him off. “I’m going to put together a bouquet with white lilacs, which represents innocence, and peonies for bashfulness and a few freesias.”

Liam’s jaw dropped. Tiffany had come very close to describing Charity’s personality. “I’ll take them.”

“Do you want a large or small bouquet?”

“I’ll let you know once you begin putting it together.”

Crossing his arms over his chest, he watched Tiffany open the door to the chilled compartment and take out an armload of stems. The sweet fragrance from the flowers wafted to his nostrils. Although he hadn't made plans to go out with Charity, he hoped she would appreciate him showing up unexpectedly with the flowers.

He'd found himself intrigued as Tiffany's gloved fingers groomed the flowers, removing the leaves and bruised or brown petals and florets. Then she placed a few stems in her hand.

"This is a small bouquet."

Liam pointed to the flowers on the table. "You can make it larger."

Tiffany worked quickly, adding more flowers until there was a free-form round bouquet with lilacs all around the edge. She added stems of freesia whenever there was a space between the peonies and lilacs, bound them together with a rubber band before cutting the stems to allow them to absorb water.

"What color ribbon would you like?"

Liam stared at spools of ribbons in different widths and colors. "Blue."

Tiffany smiled. "Light, medium or dark? Baby blue, cobalt, robin's egg, royal, periwinkle, cornflower—"

"Robin's egg!" he practically shouted, cutting off Tiffany from listing the different shades of blue.

She gave him a comforting smile. "It will be a lot easier for you to make a decision the next time you come to buy flowers for her."

"I hope you're right," he said under his breath.

She wrapped the flowers in pale blue cellophane and tied the bouquet with streamers of curling ribbon. "Do you want to include a card?"

"No, thank you." He planned to deliver them personally. He tapped his credit card on the card reader, thanked Tiffany for her assistance and walked to his vehicle. Liam had noticed surreptitious glances directed at him holding the bouquet. He wanted to tell the lookie-loos that he hadn't purchased the flowers as a make-up gesture. That he was giving them to his girlfriend who he was beginning to like more than he could've imagined.

Liam arrived at the Sanchez house, rang the bell and when the door opened came face-to-face with Marisa. She stared at him, then the bouquet of flowers. "I didn't know you cared," she teased, grinning.

"I do, Marisa, but these happen to be for Charity."

"They're exquisite, but unfortunately Charity isn't here. She left early this morning to drive back to Bronco. She's involved with an upcoming military fundraiser, and she had to meet with the committee to finalize a few things. Come in, and I'll put the flowers in water."

Liam handed Marisa the bouquet, finding odd that Charity hadn't mentioned anything to him about her involvement in a military fundraiser. Perhaps, he thought, she didn't want to remind him of anything military-related because of what he'd recently gone through. "I just stopped by to give Charity the flowers. I'll give her a call sometime tomorrow."

"Liam?"

"What?"

"If you hurt Charity, I will break your fingers."

He went completely still. "What are you talking about?"

"You and Charity."

"What about us, Marisa?" Liam was hard-pressed to keep a thread of annoyance out of his voice.

"I was just kidding about breaking your fingers, but I want to warn you that Charity's parents may not approve of you being with their daughter. Mimi and Randall did everything they could to come between me and Dawson, and they almost broke us up for good."

"And why would they want to do that?"

"Because they're social climbers, Liam. They want to pick and choose who their children should marry, and unfortunately for me, I didn't have the right pedigree."

Liam didn't want to believe what Marisa was talking about. "But you married Dawson."

"Dawson and I married each other. Things are better now between me and my in-laws to the point where they're at least cordial. So, if you continue to date Charity, then you should expect a fight from her parents. And if you're not all in, then you should walk away now before people get hurt."

Marisa had warned him to expect a fight, when for him it would become a battle if he continued to see Charity. He liked Charity. No, he adored her, and somehow, he could not imagine walking away and giving up that easily. He'd been a soldier, trained to fight and to win battles, and his sole focus had been winning. But if came to fighting for Charity and he won, then Liam knew she would eventually become the loser once she discovered how broken he was.

"I'm not going to walk away because you're telling me the Johns won't approve of me dating their daughter. I'm not one to cut and run, Marisa. I didn't do it as a soldier, and I won't do it now. If something happens and Charity decides she no longer wants to be with me, then I'll accept that without questioning her. Not with you telling me some third or fourth party doesn't want us to be together."

Marisa slowly blinked. "Are you in love with her?"

The question hit Liam as if he'd taken a direct hit to

his jaw. Was he in love with Charity John? If not in love, then was he falling in love with her? And when he thought about it, he realized there were the classic signs that bore it out. He was seeing her every day, now he was bringing her flowers. He'd kissed her, albeit chastely, but he was the one who'd initiated the kiss. Even the topic of them possibly sleeping together had been discussed, along with Charity admitting her future plan was to become a rancher's wife.

"I don't know what it is," he admitted quietly. "There are so many things I like about her, Marisa. I've never met someone like Charity. She can be worldly and innocent at the same time, and it's the innocence that makes me want to protect her. I know she wants to control her own life, yet she's not ready to sever the ties that bind her to her parents, and I don't intend to be the one who will force her or be responsible for her making that decision."

"Are you willing to fight for her?"

A beat passed. "Yes, but only if Charity wants to be with me."

"What if she doesn't?" Marisa asked.

"Then, I'll walk away."

"Even if you love her, Liam?"

A wry smile parted his lips. "Yes. Even if I love her. Charity shouldn't be forced to either be with me or adhere to her parents' wishes. In a situation like that there are no winners, only losers for all involved."

"I'm so sorry I brought this up, but I felt compelled to warn you because I know what's going to happen once Mimi and Randall discover you're dating Charity. And I would appreciate it if what I just told you stays between us."

"It's okay, Marisa. I won't say anything to Charity," he promised. Regardless of what would occur between him and the Johns, Liam didn't want Charity to become collateral damage in what could possibly become an untenable family crisis.

He drove back to the Double M, replaying his encounter with Marisa and her warning about his dating Charity. He'd joked about getting her pregnant and her parents coming for him, unaware how close he'd come to the truth. Charity was the baby of the family and the only girl, and it was apparent the Johns had big plans for their daughter which included her marrying someone they deemed acceptable. And he was glad Marisa told him about what he could possibly encounter from Charity's parents because it forced him to acknowledge what he'd denied from the first time he saw her at Dean Valentini's funeral.

There had been a connection. One so strong that he wasn't able to explain it, and it had become even stronger with each encounter.

Liam could honestly say he'd never been in love; however, whatever he felt with Charity was so different from what he'd experienced with other women that it had to be love. Liam promised Marisa what she'd told him would stay between the two of them, yet he had to talk to someone. And he knew just the person he trusted most.

Liam had sent his father a text asking him to meet him at his cabin later that night. He'd shared dinner with his family, and he'd managed to temper some of the concern that continued to plague him following his conversation with Marisa when listening to his brothers talk about the Dinosaur Day rodeo that had been so successful that rumor had it the residents were asking town officials to host the event every year. It was obvious the residents of Tenacity were ready to celebrate a new month-long event.

Harley emitted a low growl as the sweep of a vehicle's

headlight pierced the night, and Liam stood up and waited for Jack to join him on the porch. “Do you want to sit out here and talk or go inside?” Liam asked his father.

“Outside’s good.” Jack sank down to a cushioned rocker. “Why the cryptic code and the covert meeting?”

Liam sat on a facing rocker. “I didn’t want Mami to see what I’d sent you, then begin asking you countless questions you wouldn’t be able to answer.”

Leaning forward and sandwiching his hands between his knees, Jack gave him a lengthy stare. There was enough illumination coming from the porch lights for Liam to notice lines of tension bracketing his father’s mouth. “Are you having flashbacks again?”

He shook his head. “No. I haven’t had one in a while.”

“How long is a while, son?”

“I had one the first night I came back. I can honestly say it was less traumatizing than those I’d had in the past. I wanted to talk to you about something that has nothing to do with my PTSD.”

“Okay. Shoot.”

“When did you know for certain that you were in love with my mother?”

Slumping back in the rocker, Jack ran a hand over his face as he chuckled. “Really, Liam?”

“Yes, really, Dad.”

Jack lowered his hand. “I’m sorry about laughing, but whoever she is has to be mighty special for you to ask me to get out of my bed at midnight.”

“I didn’t realize she was until earlier today.” Liam told him everything, beginning with Marisa Sanchez-John’s warning about his dating Charity and the possible fallout from her parents because they wouldn’t think he was a suitable match for their daughter.

"Do you think you're in love with this girl?"

"I don't know, Dad. It's something I've been asking myself. If I'd known her longer, then I would have to say yes. But the first time I laid eyes on her was at the military funeral the same day I came home." He paused. "It probably sounds crazy, but I felt an instant connection with her, and then it happened again the next day at the dig."

"It's not crazy, Liam, because people can have a way of connecting when they least expect it. It was that way with me and your mother. I used to hang out in the Social Club after classes, and one day your mother walked in with some of her friends. I smiled at her, and I was shocked when she smiled back because she was one of the prettiest girls in the school and dudes were doing anything they could to get her attention. When I finally got up enough nerve to talk to her, I said something that was so asinine that I knew I'd doomed every chance of her going out with me."

"How old were you, and what did you say?"

Jack huffed. "Sixteen. I told her that one day she was going to marry me."

Throwing back his head, Liam laughed with abandon as Harley raised his head to look at him. "That was so cheesy. What did she say?"

"Cheesy or not, it worked because she gave me a one-word reply."

"Which was?"

"Maybe."

"Are you saying that at sixteen she actually was thinking about marrying you?"

"Yup. And six years later it became a reality. Initially her parents were against her marrying straight out of college, but once she told her father that we were planning to elope he finally gave his approval."

"But is it that important to get someone else's approval to date or marry when you don't need their permission?"

"It's very important, Liam, because when you marry it's not just your spouse but their entire family. And what if you have children? You don't want them to grow up with divided loyalties. You claim this girl's family—"

"Her name is Charity John, Dad. Her parents own the Double J in Bronco Heights."

"She comes from money." Jack's query was a statement.

"Lots of money," Liam confirmed.

"And they probably think that any man who dates their daughter is a gold-digger."

"Apparently not the wealthy ones."

"Wealthy people insist on prenups." Jack closed his eyes for several seconds. "The only advice I'm going to give you is if you love Charity, then you have to be prepared to fight for her. She has to know that you're there for her despite whatever she has to go through with her parents. They may even resort to disinheriting her."

"I'm not after her money, Dad. And if they do cut her off financially then she can come and live with me. But I'm afraid of exposing her to what I'm going through with my PTSD. I would never forgive myself for pulling her down where she has to witness my nightmares."

"Have you thought that perhaps being with her can be what you need to lift you up? And your talk about living together. With or without the promise of marriage?"

"Come on now, Dad. You should know me better than that. Of course I'd marry her."

"Well, that's something that should make your mama really happy. Now, when are we going to meet your girlfriend?"

"She's in Bronco. I'll ask her when she gets back if she wants to come to the fish fry or cookout."

"Hell, son. Invite her to both. She just might like the Double M better than her Double J."

"I think Mami has gotten to you."

"How so?" Jack questioned.

"She can't stop talking about her sons getting married and giving her grandchildren."

"Just make certain that doesn't happen before I surprise her with our thirty-fifth-wedding-anniversary celebration."

"For you information, Charity and I haven't slept together."

"That is entirely too much information." Jack pushed off the rocker, Liam also rising. "I'm glad we had this talk. Now, if the Johns decide to get funky because my son is dating their daughter, then they're going to be in a world of hurt."

"As long as it's only feelings," Liam mumbled under his breath.

"Don't sorry, son. It won't become more than a war of words." Jack rested a hand on Liam's shoulder. "Your girlfriend is a lot luckier than your mother because she doesn't have to share you with a jealous mistress. The military."

Liam hadn't thought of the military as a mistress—to which he was obligated to twenty-four seven. "Thanks, Dad, for lending you ear for me to unload on you."

"You weren't unloading, Liam. You wanted advice, and I tried to give it to you. One of these days your son will come to you when he needs advice the same way I did with my father."

Crossing his arms over his chest, he stood there until his father drove away. Liam wondered if he'd spoken too soon about inviting Charity to come live with him if her parents decided to cut her off financially. After all, she did have the option of living with her brother and sister-in-law on their ranch. And he was still was reluctant for her to witness his nightmares where images of the exploding bomb and the aftermath would result in him waking up screaming and shaking uncontrollably. If they were to sleep under the same roof, then it would have to be in separate bedrooms.

"Harley? Are you coming in or sleeping out?" The shepherd stood up, shook himself, then headed for the door when Liam opened it. "I suppose you're going to stick close to home now because you don't want a repeat encounter with those skunks."

Liam walked up the staircase, leaving Harley on his bed next to the table in the entrance. He wondered if he hadn't bought the flowers and taken them to the Sanchez home whether Marisa would've been as forthcoming about his relationship with Charity. She'd questioned if he loved Charity, and so had his father.

He'd had asked himself the same question, and now he knew the answer. With each passing day he did find himself falling in love with her.

Chapter Ten

"Dawson?"

"That's my name."

Charity glared at her brother who hadn't taken his eyes off a binder filled with his ranch's financial reports and construction updates. "It's the second time I've called your name, and will you please permit me a few minutes of your time because I need to discuss something with you?"

Dawson John's head popped up, and he ran a hand through tousled dusty-blond hair, his blue eyes meeting those of his sister's. "Okay, sis. You have my undivided attention."

"I want to talk to you about our parents."

"What about them?"

"I've met someone I really like."

"And?"

She huffed. "I don't think Mom and Dad are going to like him."

"Because his folks aren't members of the Association?"

"Dawson! I'm serious."

"So am I, Charity. The only reason you want to discuss your boyfriend with me is because he probably doesn't have at least seven figures attached to his family's name."

"How did you know?"

"Because I know our parents. They can't stop competing with the Taylors and Abernathys—especially when it comes to who their children marry. Whenever I talk to Mom, she's always mentioning that she's found a nice young man she would like to introduce you to."

"I found a nice young man."

Dawson smiled, and attractive lines fanned out around his sparkling blue eyes. "The young man who brought you flowers yesterday?" He angled his head. "Liam Martin?"

Charity nodded. The day before she had left Tenacity for Bronco to sit in on a meeting to finalize the plans for a fundraiser. She would've returned to Tenacity later that afternoon if Mimi hadn't requested Charity join her for dinner at the Association. It was close to midnight when she finally made it back to Tenacity, too late for her to contact Liam to thank him for the exquisite bouquet.

"Yes," she confirmed. "Liam Martin. Please don't tell me you don't approve of me seeing him."

Dawson's eyebrows slanted in a frown. "I can't believe you would say something like that after what I had to go through before I married Marisa."

Charity bit her lip and dropped her eyes. "I'm sorry, Dawson. I didn't mean for it to come out like that." She shook her head. "I'm falling in love with a man I didn't know existed two weeks ago."

"Don't you think it's too soon for you to talk about being in love? It's probably more like infatuation."

"Is that what you really think? That I'm confusing infatuation with love?"

Dawson leaned back, giving her a long penetrating stare. "I can't get into your head. Therefore, I don't know what you're thinking, Charity."

"I know Mom and Dad gave you a hard time once you

started dating Marisa, but now that they've accepted her, I figure it will go easier for me once I introduce them to Liam. He's former military, and he comes from a good family. And it doesn't matter that he's not from Bronco Heights."

Dawson huffed and shook his head. "I know they still see you as their youngest child and only daughter, so it's difficult for them to relate to you any differently. And I'm included in that equation, Charity. It's still hard for me to see you as a grown woman when I've always thought of you as a little girl."

Charity glared at her brother. "I can assure you that I am a grown woman. One who knows what she wants and what she doesn't want. And if our parents make me choose between them and Liam, then I'm going to choose Liam."

"Are you really serious? You claim you haven't known him long, and now you're willing to choose someone who's practically a stranger over your parents?"

"They would react the same way if Liam and I were dating for years. And you're a fine one to talk about not knowing someone long. How long did it take for you to fall for Marisa?"

"It was different with me."

"How, brother?"

"Firstly, I was older than you, and secondly I'd dated enough women to know what I wanted."

"Age has nothing to do with it, Dawson. I know who I am and who I want in my life. And right now, it's Liam Martin."

A beat passed. "You really love him, don't you?"

Charity struggled not to cry. "Yes. I don't know what it is, but whenever I'm with him I feel safe. That's something I never felt with any guy I dated."

"Maybe it's because he was military."

She shook her head. “I don’t think it’s that. He’s calm, gentle, and I’m always completely relaxed around him. I feel comfortable enough to say whatever is on my mind without having to censor myself. And when I do say something he’s not merely hearing me, he’s also listening.”

“He sounds like a great guy.”

“He is, Dawson. Marisa says he’s an old family friend, so if you want to know more about my boyfriend, then you should ask her. Speaking of asking, I’m going to ask Liam to be my date for the Presents for Patriots fundraiser in Bronco.”

“Good luck with that,” Dawson said under his breath.

Charity rolled her eyes at her brother. “Do you plan on coming to witness everyone’s reaction when I show up with him?”

“Nah. I’m going to Cheyenne to bid on some horses.”

“The stables are magnificent, by the way. Marisa gave me a tour.” The structure contained sophisticated heating and cooling systems and wired security.

Dawson smiled. “Now that they’re completed, it’s time for my agent to purchase some quality horseflesh.”

“Good luck.”

Charity was wishing her brother luck when realistically she knew she would need it once she introduced Liam to her parents.

Liam turned off the local road and onto one leading to the Double M. He gave Charity a quick sidelong glance and found her staring out the side window at the passing landscape. He’d taken his father’s advice and invited Charity to the Double M for a late-Friday-afternoon fish fry. She’d accepted, then asked what she should bring, laughing when he told her just herself. It was apparent she’d ignored him because when he picked up her at the Sanchez house, she was carrying two large canvas bags she claimed were filled with stuff.

"Your fence posts look new."

"They are. My father and brothers replaced all of them earlier this year."

"That's a never-ending job for cattle ranchers or horse farmers," she stated.

"Ranching and farming are never-ending operations," Liam countered. "You have to be up at dawn to either milk cows, gather eggs, groom horses, muck out stalls, cut grass and bale hay. Then it's herding horses or cattle to where they can graze. In other words, it's not a nine-to-fiver where you can take coffee breaks or clock out once the work day is over."

"You don't break for meals?"

Liam smiled. "We Martins break for breakfast, lunch and dinner. My mother is up before five making breakfast. Then we come back to the main house around noon for lunch. Dinner is always between six and seven."

"She cooks three meals a day?"

"Yup. That's something she wants to do. My father told her she could pack lunches for us and we could eat in-between chores, but Maria Martin wasn't having it. Her mandate is come home, wash up and sit down to eat as a family."

"I like her mandate."

"You do?"

"Yes, Liam. Eating lunch sitting on the ground or in the flatbed of a pickup is crazy."

"Where do your ranch hands eat?"

"There's a bunkhouse and kitchen on the property for them where a cook prepares their meals."

"There's a main house and kitchen on the Double M, where a cook, who happens to be Maria Martin, prepares all of our meals."

Charity narrowed her eyes. "What are you trying to say?"

"I'm not trying to say anything, Charity, but there is little difference between the Double M and J. The exception is the size and scope of the operation."

Charity wanted to tell Liam there was a marked difference between the two ranches and it had to do with their parents. Although she hadn't been introduced to Jack and Maria Martin she doubted whether they would treat her with the same contempt Randall and Mimi John had with Marisa once they realized she was dating Dawson.

She knew she couldn't change her parents who sought to pick and choose who they wanted their children to marry. They were who they are, and like her brothers, the final decision as to who she wanted to be with rested with her.

"Have your brothers invited their girlfriends to the fish fry?"

"Nope."

"Why not?"

"Because my brothers claim they're on breaks from dating."

"I don't understand couples who claim to be on break."

"What don't you understand?"

"I believe it's just an excuse to cheat. And once they discover the grass isn't any greener on the other side they come slinking back."

"Why do they have to slink, Charity?"

"Because that's what men do. It happens all the time

with athletes and entertainers. They know what they have yet somehow can't resist temptation."

"Is that what happened to you and someone you dated?" Liam asked.

"No, but it did happen to one of my college roommates. Her fiancé told her he wanted a break because he wasn't certain whether he wanted to be a father. She agreed to the break, and seven months later they reconciled after he said he'd changed his mind about wanting children. Meanwhile, she hadn't known that he'd been fooling around with an old girlfriend and gotten her pregnant."

"When did she find out about the baby?"

"He told her on their honeymoon."

"Oh shit! I'm sorry about that," Liam apologized.

Charity sucked her tongue and teeth. "You don't have to apologize because I grew up around brothers who could fill a swear jar to overflowing every other day. If we had one."

"Did she end up staying with him?"

"No! She called her father from Hawaii and told him to make arrangements to fly her back to the mainland, then for him to contact their family lawyer so she could file for an annulment."

"So, Mister Break ended up on the losing end."

"Big time."

"Good for her."

"You're taking her side?"

"Why wouldn't I take her side, Charity?"

"I thought dudes always stick together."

Liam shook his head. "Not when they take advantage of women. I don't have a sister, but if I did and some knucklehead decided to mess with her, then it would be lights out for him."

Charity stared at Liam's profile. "What would you do to him?"

"You don't want to know."

Their conversation ended when Liam drove around to the rear of a large two-story house and came to a stop. Charity didn't know what to expect, but it wasn't the sprawling ranch-style home with a deck and patio. A picnic table and benches were set up under a gazebo in the expansive backyard.

Liam cut off the engine, and rested his right hand on her left forearm. "I'll get your stuff, then I'll introduce you to my family."

Charity met his eyes. "I know you told me not to bring anything, but I thought fresh fruit would be nice for dessert."

Leaning to his right, he kissed her. "You're all the dessert I need."

"Didn't anyone tell you that you're too old to make out in a vehicle? Get a room, bro!"

Liam shifted, glaring at Enzo grinning at him through the open driver's window. "For your information, I have quite a few rooms. Please come around and help Charity while I get the bags from the back."

His brother witnessing him kissing Charity wasn't something Liam had wanted to advertise. And there was no doubt Enzo had embarrassed her because pinpoints of color dotted her cheeks. He got out and lifted both bags, then rounded the pickup to find Enzo introducing himself to Charity.

Liam didn't want to believe his older brother—who women found almost impossible to resist and who recently claimed he was through with women—was smiling at his girlfriend. And judging from Charity's expression, she was eating it up.

"Easy with my woman, bro."

"No need to worry, little brother. I was just asking Charity what she would like to eat."

"Just checking," Liam said, smiling. Tonight, would be the first fish fry he would celebrate with his family in nearly two years, and having Charity join in would make it even more memorable.

Liam introduced Charity to the rest of his family, and she appeared slightly overwhelmed when greeted with embraces from his father and Marco, and a kiss from his mother, before they began setting up what promised to become hours of feasting on fish, salads, mild and piquant sauces and an assortment of liquid refreshment including beer, pop, lemonade and sparkling water. Charity had contributed two large bowls of freshly cut watermelon, cantaloupe, honeydew, blueberries and strawberries, kiwi and green grapes. Maria had thanked Charity for the fruit, saying it was the perfect dessert to offset the richness of the fried fish.

"Are you okay?" he whispered into her ear.

"I'm more than okay. Your family is wonderful."

He leaned closer, his shoulder brushing hers. "I like them, too."

"Liam..."

"What is it, sweetheart?"

"I don't think you realize how lucky you are."

"Yeah, I do. I'm lucky to have met you."

Charity shook her head. "I'm talking about your family. I just met them, and I feel the same connection with them as I do with you."

Liam winked at her. "That's because we were destined to

be together because we both were connected to Dean Valentini." Reaching for Charity's hand, he led her to a clearing where Enzo had set up the outdoor fryer. A half dozen trays of marinated fish lined a nearby table.

Charity stared at the table. "There's enough fish here to feed a football team."

Enzo, wearing a fireproof glove, inserted a thermometer from the side of the cooker to test the oil's temperature. "And I'm willing to bet there won't be any leftovers."

She tucked several strands behind an ear that had escaped her ponytail. "The fish smells delicious even before it's cooked."

"That's because it was marinated overnight in a secret blend of spices, then coated in finely ground seasoned cornmeal and corn starch," Enzo explained.

Liam rested his hand at the small of Charity's back. "Enzo is a fish-frying Picasso."

Tilting her chin, she smiled up at him. "You can stay here and watch Picasso paint his masterpiece while I go see if I can help your mother finish setting up."

He watched Charity walk away, then turned to see Enzo staring at him. "What?"

Enzo gave him a half smile. "I have to give it to you, brother. You hit the jackpot with Charity."

Liam's eyebrows lifted questioningly. "So, you like her."

"Yes, because she's nothing like I'd imagined she would be."

"And that is?"

"A spoiled little rich girl."

"She's the complete opposite."

Even before he'd become aware of who Charity John was, Liam never would've taken her for a spoiled rich girl. There was nothing about her appearance or demeanor indicating she came from money, aside from her driving a vehicle with a six-figure price tag. There was no doubt her clothes were expensive but not ostentatious, and her only jewelry was a tiny pair of diamonds studs. She might have been Bronco Heights elite, yet she'd managed to blend in rather than stand out among the residents of Tenacity.

"What are you doing to do about it?" Enzo questioned as he put several pieces of fish in the boiling oil.

"Do about what?"

"Is it serious between the two of you?"

Liam stared at the toes of his boots. "Define *serious*, Enzo."

"Do you find it hard to breathe whenever you're around her, or do you go to bed and wake up thinking about her?"

"You need to stop hanging out with Mami whenever she's watching those damned telenovelas."

Enzo chuckled. "She told you about that?"

"She sort of mentioned it in passing."

"I watch them with her whenever Dad stays in Billings for a couple of days. I know she's recalling the times when he was serving and away from home. That couldn't have been easy for her, Liam, even though *abuela* came to live with us to help Mami."

"But Mami knew he'd planned on a military career even before she married Dad."

"True, but people change, Liam. Maybe if she hadn't had kids, then maybe she would've been content to live on base with him. Dad wanted to be a soldier and Mami wanted to be a teacher, and that was something she wasn't willing to give up."

"She didn't give up her career, but he was forced to give up his," Liam argued. However, he'd compromised by becoming a reservist.

Enzo picked up a spatula, scooped several pieces of crusty golden fried fish out of the oil and placed them to drain on a wire rack covered with paper towels. "That was a sacrifice he was willing to make to save his marriage. Couples do it every day."

Liam stared at his brother. "Is that what happened to you, Enzo? She wasn't willing to compromise to save your relationship?"

Enzo glared at him, giving Liam what he thought of as a death stare. "I meant what I said when I told you I don't want to talk about it."

Liam held up both hands. "There's no need to get hostile," he said, backpedaling. "I just want you to know that I'm here for you if or when you ever feel comfortable enough to talk about it. Man to man. Brother to brother."

"What you need to do is go rescue your girlfriend before our mother convinces her to set a wedding date so she can become an *abuela* and me a *tío*."

Liam wanted to tell his brother he was hallucinating. Liam knew he wasn't the one to make his mother's dreams a reality because his relationship with Charity wasn't one based on longevity. He was realistic enough to believe there would come a time when she would return to Bronco to stay. She'd asked if he would be her date for a Bronco Heights military fundraiser, and he'd agreed, well aware it would probably be their last time together. He would return to Tenacity, and she would go back to her life on the Double J.

Liam sat on the bench with his brothers opposite Charity who sat between his parents. Platters of fried fish, bowls of spicy Asian slaw and pasta salad were passed around the table. Maria's remoulade and tartar sauce, along with bottles of hot sauce were available for dousing or dipping crunchy, perfectly seasoned seafood.

Charity touched a napkin to the corners of her mouth. “I can’t believe y’all do this every Friday.”

“We try most Fridays whenever the weather decides to cooperate,” Jack said, smiling.

Marco cocked his head and stared at his father. “Dad, you know we don’t have fish-fry Fridays when you’re out of town.”

Liam elbowed Marco in the ribs when he saw Jack’s angry expression. Even though he’d been away from home for years he was aware of the undercurrent of friction between his parents whenever their father spent time away from the ranch.

“Let it go,” he warned Marco under his breath.

Jack glared at Marco. “If I’m out of town, it’s to make extra money to buy that fancy little sports car you wanted for your birthday so you can impress your honeys.”

Marco frowned. “Damn, Dad. Why did you have to call them honeys?”

“Because you call every woman sweetie,” Jack countered. “And isn’t honey sweet?”

Maria rested a hand over her husband’s. “Jack, please. We have company.”

Jack turned to Charity. “Are you company or Liam’s girlfriend?”

A smile flitted across Charity’s delicate features. “I guess I’m his honey, because he also called me sweetheart.”

The tension was shattered by unrestrained laughter from those sitting at the table, and in that instant Liam discovered Charity could easily fit into his world. Not only had she charmed him but also his family. And he hadn’t been aware he’d called her the endearment until now.

Marco raised his mug of beer and winked at Charity. "To Miss Charity John. Welcome to the family."

Liam went completely still as Marco's pronouncement was echoed by the others. Reacting in slow motion, he finally hoisted his glass and met Charity eyes that were shimmering with excitement. Did she want to become a member of his family even though Marisa had warned him that hers would never accept him? Suddenly he felt like a fraud when he was forced to smile with the others.

I have to let it go and not dwell on the fact that Charity might be forced to choose between me and her parents. And there is one thing I refuse to do, and that's come between them, no more than I'd want to be in a situation where I'd have to choose between her and my family. Maybe it's best that she's only going to be in Tenacity for another week.

Liam managed to shake off his uneasiness as he ate, drank and traded jokes with his brothers about their childhood antics where they'd believed they'd managed to fool their parents. The sun had set, and solar lights along the perimeter of the backyard illuminated the area, attracting bugs, signaling it was time to clean up and head indoors.

Wrapping an arm around Charity's waist, he led her to his vehicle. "I'm going to make one stop before I take you home."

She rested her head on his shoulder. "Where we going?"

He dropped a kiss on her hair. "To my place. It's time for Harley to meet my special friend."

The rush of excitement that quickened Charity's pulse when Liam mentioned taking her to his home vanished quickly. She'd spent an amazing time with him and his family, and spending the night with him at his house would've become the perfect ending to a perfect day. She knew he was reluctant to make love to her, and she was more than willing to wait until the time was right for them to take their relationship to another level.

"Does Harley stay in the house when you're not there?" she asked, securing her seat belt.

"He does at night. I let him out during the day, where he hangs out with the other herding dogs."

"Is he herding cattle with the other dogs?"

Liam laughed softly. "No. He's now their pack leader, so most times they end up either chasing one another or finding a cool spot to sleep whenever it gets too hot."

"Has he retained the instincts of a military dog?"

"That's something he'll never forget."

When she first saw the magnificent black-and-tan dog standing motionless at Liam's side, she'd found him intimidating. "Will I be able to pet him?"

"I wouldn't recommend it until he's completely relaxed around you. He's been hanging out at my mother's house, and it took a couple of days before he would approach her. This is a first for my mother because as kids she would never allow us to bring animals into her home. I believe it was because of an incident when I'd found an injured fox kit and brought it home for her take care of its wounds. Mami screamed as if someone had stabbed her, and I was so frightened that I dropped the kit and it ran around the kitchen looking to escape."

"Shame on you, Liam. How old were you when you traumatized your mother?"

"I was around four and I wanted to be a veterinarian, so I was always looking to take care of injured birds and other wildlife."

"And there's no doubt that you still like animals because you became a dog handler."

"Harley and I are partners and best buds."

You have Harley, but are you willing to make room in your life for another partner? One not of the canine persuasion.

Charity had tried and failed, but she couldn't stop thinking about sharing not only her life but also her future with Liam Martin. She was willing to give him all the time he needed to fall in love with her, because she knew unequivocally that she was falling in love with him. She'd watched his reaction when his family had welcomed her into their family, and she'd felt her heart stop before it began beating again when he'd hesitated joining their toast.

Liam stopped in front of a cabin that was a smaller replica of the one his parents occupied yet was bigger than what she'd anticipated. "How big is your home?"

"It's half the size of the main house."

"A number in square feet, Liam."

"Twenty-eight hundred."

"That's not what I'd call a cabin." She didn't tell him that the cabins on Dawson's ranch averaged half of that.

"The main house was expanded several times because prior generations of Martins had large families who all tended to live under one roof. Then to alleviate the overcrowding they began building the cabins. We all have our cabins, and there are two others on the property for when we host family reunions." He cut off the engine. "Are you ready to meet the boss of the house?"

Charity smiled. "Yes, sir." She waited for Liam to get out and come around to assist her down.

"Wait here on the porch, and I'll bring him out."

She sat on the steps of the porch, staring up at the millions of stars littering the clear nighttime sky. A knowing smile parted her lips as she realized it had been a while since she'd enjoyed just being herself and not Double J's ranch heiress.

"Don't move or turn around," Liam said quietly. "Harley's not dangerous, but he's somewhat cautious when meeting new people."

Charity sucked in her breath, then slowly let it out when she felt the dog beside her on the step. He nuzzled her shoulder, then sat close to her. She saw out of the corner of her eye Liam fold his body down, with Harley sitting between them. Then, without warning, Harley rested his muzzle on her thigh, silently communicating he had accepted with her.

"I think Harley just found a new friend," she said, smiling.

"You must have some special mojo, because he doesn't usually take to anyone this quickly."

"It's not mojo, Liam. It's because Harley knows we have a special connection with each other."

"You think?"

"I know. I hope you're planning to bring him to next week's military fundraiser."

Liam rested a hand on Harley's back. "I'm really looking forward to it." He wondered if Charity's involvement in the fundraising had anything to do with her briefly dating Dean. And as former military any attempt to support veterans made Charity even more special when it came to their relationship.

Chapter Eleven

Charity felt as if something was conspiring against her when she was forced to return to Bronco to meet with the fundraising committee because one of the members had neglected to finalize ordering audio-visual equipment for the event.

She spent hours on the computer searching for companies, then calling to see if they had anyone available to come and set up before the weekend. If the committee had arranged to have the event at the Bronco Convention Center, then it would've been no problem, but Chuck Carter, the center's manager, told her it had been booked solid for the rest of the month.

"Charity, darling, you're going to have to take a break from staring at that computer and eat something."

Charity glanced over at her mother, who stood in the doorway of the office where she conducted Double J business. "I will once I find a company willing to come and set up for the fundraiser."

Mimi walked into the office. "You've spent the past three days tapping keys and returning phone calls. Why don't you let it go for now? We can go to the Association for lunch and get you out of the house for a couple of hours."

It's you who likes to lunch at the Association, not me.

And I don't want to pretend to smile at those fake-ass women who believe they were better born and better bred than those who live and work in Bronco Valley. If it wasn't for many of them marrying up, then they wouldn't be lunching or dining at the club.

"No, thanks, Mom. I'll fix something for myself."

Mimi gave her a critical look. "I don't know what it is, Charity, but I sense a change in you every time you come back from Tenacity. I hope you're not thinking about moving there. It's enough that Dawson decided to give up his life on the Double J to purchase a rundown ranch that will take several generations before it could even come close to what he could've had here."

Swiveling on the executive chair, Charity struggled not to explode and tell her mother exactly what was on her mind. "Have you ever considered that Dawson doesn't want what you want for him? It began with his dating Marisa, and now it's his decision to build his own ranch."

"But why should he spend his time and money to set up a ranch when he could live on the Double J?"

Maybe it is because he had to get away from you and Dad trying to control his life. "Have you thought that perhaps he wants to be his own man? Build a legacy with his wife and the children they hope to have?"

Mimi frowned. "Where is all of this talk coming from, Charity? I know you're fond of Marisa, but is she saying things about me that are turning you against me?"

Charity smiled in spite of the seriousness of their conversation. "It's not always about you, Mother."

"Oh, now it's *Mother*?"

"You are my mother, aren't you?"

"Yes. But you never call me that. It sounds so detached and unemotional."

"It's how girls of a certain social class address their mothers, because *Mom* or *Mama* sound so common."

Mimi's eyes narrowed. "Something tells me you're spoiling for a fight, and I don't intend to oblige you, so if you want to eat, then you know where the kitchen is."

Charity closed her eyes, feeling as if she'd just gone a few mental rounds with her mother. She didn't know why Mimi refused to accept what she wanted wasn't the same thing her children wanted. And if she didn't stop competing with the Taylors and Abernathys, then she would never appreciate what she'd been given. She and Randall owned one of the largest ranches in Bronco Heights, were members of an exclusive country club and were among the social elite, yet it still wasn't enough. Mimi wasn't spoiling for a fight, yet Charity knew there would be a fight and fireworks once her mother discovered her daughter was dating a man from Tenacity.

Liam hadn't realized how much he'd missed seeing Charity until she returned to Tenacity after she'd spent five days in Bronco. She was able to contract the services of an audio-visual company in a small town hundreds of miles from Bronco by offering to cover the cost of their travel and also securing reservations at the Heights Hotel for their technicians to stay before and after the event.

Cradling her face in his hands, Liam brushed a light kiss on her mouth. "You look as if you've been burning the candle at both ends." There were dark smudges under her large blue eyes.

"If this event wasn't so important for Bronco veterans, I would've suggested we cancel it."

"But not at the expense of your running yourself into the ground, sweetheart."

She smiled. "Sweet like honey?"

Liam winked. "Sweeter. I know you talked about planning to stay in Bronco after the fundraiser, so I hope you don't mind if I change your plans."

"Why?"

"Instead of you driving to Bronco, I'll take you there in my truck and bring you back. After you get some rest, then you should be able to drive yourself without falling asleep behind the wheel."

As if on cue, Charity put up her hand to smother a yawn. "I like your plan. I only came back because I wanted to see you, and it's been a while since I've been able to go to sleep and not wake up thinking about the fundraiser."

"And I'm glad to see you, too. One more day, then it's all behind you."

He kissed her again, increasing the pressure until her lips parted. He showered kisses around her lips and along her jaw and the column of her scented neck. It was as if he wanted to brand her with his mouth, because in another twenty-four hours they would be left with only memories of each other. That is, if she decided to stay in Bronco.

Liam lowered his hands, turned on his heels, walked out of the home belonging to the Sanchezes, his heart feeling like a stone in his chest. He had two reasons for wanting to drive Charity to Bronco. It would give him more time for them to be together, and once he drove her back to Tenacity.

"You know he's in love with you, don't you?"

Charity turned to find Marisa standing a few feet away. "How long have you been standing there?"

"Long enough to hear and see what you can't. The man's in love with you, and I'm going to say this once, then I'm going to shut my pie-hole. If you don't fight for him, then you're going to regret it for the rest of your life."

Charity closed her eyes. She wanted to tell her sister-in-law at that moment she couldn't fight with or for anyone because she was mentally and emotionally drained after dealing with the fundraiser and her mother. "I know."

"I'm out," Marisa said, then pantomimed dropping a mic.

Earlier that morning Marisa had asked her to accompany her when shopping for something for her new house. She'd declined the invitation because she doubted whether she could garner enough energy to help Marisa with anything. Liam was right. She was past tired. She was exhausted.

Charity was ready for Liam when he arrived to pick her up for their drive to Bronco the next day. She'd managed to sleep more than five hours, but it still wasn't enough for her to feel alert.

She didn't wait for him to get out and assist her when she got into the Ram. Harley lay on the rear seats atop a protective covering. "Hey, buddy. I missed you."

Liam shifted into gear. "You missed him and I missed you."

"Like in the song 'Missing You' by John Waite?"

"No, bae. Those lyrics are about someone who really isn't missing someone once they are out of their life. You have to know you'll always be special to me."

Charity turned her head so he wouldn't see her eyes welling with tears. "Don't, Liam."

"Don't what?"

"Please don't make this harder on me than it needs to be."

"What are you talking about?"

"Why do I feel as if I'm losing my best friend?"

Taking his right hand off the wheel, Liam gently squeezed her thigh. "You're not losing me. It's not as if Bronco is on the other side of the country. All you have to do is send me a text and we can meet for dinner at DJ's Deluxe or you can come to Tenacity for Mexican food at Castillo's. And if you want real honkytonk, then we can go to the Grizzly Bar."

"You're right."

Charity realized she was being a Debbie Downer when Liam hadn't mentioned breaking up with her. After all, they were friends, not lovers. She gave him a sidelong glance, smiling. He wore his dog tags, tan T-shirt and fatigue pants that had been a part of his uniform during his time in the Middle East, along with the matching boots. The buckle on his belt bore the insignia of the US Army. Today he was all military, and so was Harley with his fatigue harness and lead.

Shifting, she stared out the side window for the remainder of the drive. If she hadn't been expected to attend the fundraiser, she would've asked—no, begged—Liam to stop at a motel and make nonstop love to her. And it wouldn't matter if he had protection because she felt reckless enough to defy nature; if she did become pregnant, then she would always have a piece of him in their child. She had come to love him just that much.

The area where the annual Bronco Summer Family Rodeo took place was quickly filling up with vehicles and spectators who'd paid to attend the Presents for Patriots fundraiser to benefit Bronco's former and active military. Liam parked his pickup, and Charity kissed his cheek. "I have to go and meet with the committee. I'll see you later."

Liam winked at her. "Go do your thing." When Charity

had asked him to be her date for the fundraiser, he'd teased her saying she was going to expose him to her high-society friends. She'd corrected him saying she had acquaintances, not friends, and if the fundraiser was a success, then he wondered if he could start a chapter of the foundation in Tenacity. It could be something he could do with his life because he'd been spared.

Liam sat, watching Charity until she disappeared among the crowd that had gathered. He got out, pulling the black straw Stetson lower on his forehead, then opened the rear door for Harley to jump out. He attached the lead to the shepherd's harness and walked over to the stands that were quicky filling up. Members of past and present military along with the different branches were in attendance as evidenced by their uniforms.

He was quickly garnering a lot of attention because of Harley, who'd stood motionless at his side. Liam found a place to sit at the end of one of the bleachers, then commanded Harley to sit. Sitting at the end would allow people to move past him without disturbing his dog.

A man wearing army fatigues sat next to him. "Nice dog."

"Thanks."

"You active?"

Liam shook his head. "No. Got out six months ago. You?"

"Retired, but joined the Guard last year."

"Harley and I are trying to fit into life as civvies."

"Good for you. I'm not sure how long I'm going to stay in, because the wife has been beating her gums that she's tired of me playing soldier because she can't take my mood shifts from PTSD."

"I'm going through the same thing," Liam admitted.

The row was filling with young men who appeared to have had a few drinks prior to their coming to the event. He heard one point to Charity and tell his friend that she'd beat out his cousin in the Miss Bronco Pageant several years ago.

Liam stared at Charity talking to several people who, like her, were wearing badges attached to lanyards that identified them as members of the fundraiser committee. He was once again astounded by her natural beauty. It was no doubt responsible for her becoming a pageant winner, and he wondered how many pageants she had competed in while growing up. Pageants and country clubs. She probably had participated in a coming-out celebration to introduce her to young men as a potential match for one befitting her social standing. He didn't know how close he'd come when he'd told Charity that they came from different worlds.

Charity scanned the crowd for Liam, smiling when she saw him surrounded by some of her upper-class acquaintances who no doubt were drawn to his good looks and to Harley. It was hard to resist a soldier with a dog. To say the event was a success was an understatement. The committee's treasurer proudly announced that Bronco residents were more than generous when donating monies to an organization geared to assist past and present military personnel find housing and help with mental health referrals. She walked off the stage and was making her way to Liam when she came face-to-face with her mother.

"What are you doing here?" The query came out harsher than Charity intended.

"I came to see what you'd worked so hard to put on. And I must admit it came off wonderfully."

"Thanks, Mom. I was hoping all of the sacrifice was worth it."

"It was," Mimi said, smiling. "I'm so proud of you."

"Where's Dad?"

"He's meeting some of his friends at the Association for drinks."

"And you didn't go with him?" It was a rare occasion when Mimi didn't join Randall at the private club.

"I have better things to do than sit and listen to men talk about their golfing handicaps."

Looping her arm through Mimi's, Charity steered her to where Liam was holding court with a group of admiring women. "Mom, I want you to meet my friend."

Mimi's pale eyebrows lifted slightly above the frames of her designer sunglasses. "Are you talking about the man with the dog?"

"Yes." Charity got his attention, and he excused himself and approached her. "Liam, this my mother, Mimi John. Mom, this is a very good friend of mine. Liam Martin."

Liam touched the brim of his Stetson with his free hand. "It's a pleasure to meet you, Mrs. John."

"Same here," Mimi said with a barely perceptible parting of her lips.

Charity smiled at Liam. "I need to update the few things with the committee, then I'll be ready to head back to Tenacity."

Liam nodded. "Take your time. After I take Harley for a walk I'll meet you in the parking area." He smiled at Mimi. "Again, it's nice meeting you, Mrs. John."

"Is there something going on between the two of you?" Mimi whispered once Liam was out of earshot.

Charity's eyelids fluttered wildly. "What do you mean by 'something going on'?"

"Don't insult my intelligence, Charity. I hope you're not involved with him because he's—he's..."

"He's what?" Charity questioned angrily, when her mother's words trailed off.

Mimi puffed up her chest. "Because he's all wrong for you."

"Wrong how, Mother?"

"He's poor, Charity. That's what wrong. There's no way he would be able to give you the things you take for granted. You're my daughter, my baby, and I want to give you the world. Why would you want to limit your opportunities with a poor man?"

Charity chewed her lip to keep from spewing curses. "He's hardly what you call poor. His family owns their ranch and for your information he served this country for eight years and was so severely wounded that it is a miracle that he's still alive. What if I tell you that I'm in love with him? And if he asked me to marry him, I would in a heartbeat even if he didn't have a penny to his name." Mimi clutched her chest as if she were having a heart attack, and Charity had seen the gesture enough to know there was nothing wrong with her mother's heart.

"You can't," Mimi whispered.

"I can and I will. I'm going back to Tenacity with Liam, and this is the last day I will call Bronco home."

Charity quickly walked away from Mimi because she didn't want to witness what would become staged histrionics. Enough was enough until it'd become too much. Charity didn't know how her brothers had put up with their parents' manipulation but she had no wish to do it.

Yes. She loved Liam enough to turn her back on the only lifestyle she'd known to become truly emancipated. And it didn't matter if she was cut off financially because she had enough resources to rent an apartment and provide for her necessary essentials until she was able to become gainfully employed.

It seemed like an eternity till Charity found Liam standing next to his pickup. She'd gone into a stall in a nearby bathroom and cried. And once she was back in control, she'd splashed cold water onto her face, patted it dry, then put on the sunglasses she always carried in her crossbody.

"Please take me back to Tenacity. Now, Liam."

"What's wrong?"

"I just want to leave here."

He shook his head. "Something upset you, and I'm not going to drive almost a hundred miles without you telling me what's bothering you."

"I'm done with my mother."

"What do you mean by done?"

"I won't be smothered by my parents any longer. They've controlled every aspect of my life from the time I was old enough to understand that everything to them has a price tag. And that includes love. Liam, my mother believes you're wrong for me when she knows nothing about you."

"Look, Charity, I don't want to be the cause of anything coming between you and your family."

"It's not you, Liam. It would be any man who they believe isn't wealthy enough. They've dictated who I can date or not date, and I'm sick of it. A few years back they planned to pass the family business to whichever of us married first and produced an heir."

Liam's eyebrows shot up. "That's crazy."

"That's beyond crazy, but it ends today. When I go back to Tenacity, I'm going to find an apartment and live my life without someone telling me who I should see or not see."

"Is that what you want?"

"It's what I need, Liam."

"Can't you wait and move in with your brother and Marisa once the repairs on their ranch are completed?"

She shook her head. "No, because I would be trading my mother for my brother. It's not that he'd try and control my life, but Dawson continues to treat me like his little sister rather a grown woman."

Leaning closer, Liam said, "I want you to remember one thing."

Tilting her chin, she tried to see his eyes behind the dark lenses. "What's that?"

"It doesn't matter what happens—I promise to be here for you. I also need to remind you what I've been going through with my PTSD."

Charity flashed a hint of a smile. "You told me when we first met that you wanted to make a fresh start with your life. Well, it's the same with me. And that can only happen once I move to Tenacity. But I have to ask you if you're willing take this journey with me, because you've told me what you've been going through with PTSD."

Liam opened the passenger door. "Get in, bae. It's time for you to start your new journey."

Going on tiptoe, Charity kissed him with all the passion she could summon for the man who unknowingly had stolen her heart. "Are you willing to take the journey with me?" she repeated.

Liam stared at her under lowered lids. "Yes."

Chapter Twelve

"How was the fundraiser?"

Liam sat at the breakfast island in his mother's kitchen, enjoying a cup of iced coffee. He didn't know how she did it, but everything Maria Martin cooked or brewed was delicious. "It was nice."

"Just nice?"

"Charity told me the committee raised twice the amount they'd aimed for, so it was a rousing success."

"That's good to know, because military veterans need all of the help they can get." She cut an avocado in half, tapped the pit with the blade of a knife to remove it from the fruit.

For as long as Liam could remember, Maria had been growing avocados. She'd clean the pit and suspend it over water using toothpicks, while ensuring the bottom half of the seed was submerged. Window ledges in the kitchen were lined with glasses to take advantage of the sun, and once the roots and shoots appeared she'd put them in pots with well-draining soil. His mother had become an expert in pruning and repotting the plants until they matured into trees. She'd set up a greenhouse with a southern exposure to nurture them, along with lemon and lime trees.

"I suppose you're going to miss Charity now that she's gone back to Bronco."

A beat passed. "She's not going back."

Maria's expression mirrored confusion. "I thought you told me she was going to stay in Bronco after the fund-raiser."

"That was her plan before she had a dustup with her mother."

Wiping her hands on a kitchen towel, Maria leaned over the counter. "What happened?"

Liam gave his mother an abbreviated version of what Charity told him. "She claims she's had enough of Mimi John telling her who she can or cannot date."

Maria's eyes narrowed. "I hope she wasn't talking about you."

"It could've been me, or whoever Charity went out with in the past."

"I know that woman better not be…" Maria quickly switched from English to Spanish, shocking Liam with the blistering tirade peppered with a number of profanities.

"Mami, stop. It's not that serious."

"Serious! Yeah, it is when she doesn't think my son is good enough for her daughter. And Charity's right for leaving Bronco so she can date whoever the hell she wants."

Liam swallowed a groan. He regretted telling his mother why Charity had chosen to move from Bronco to Tenacity. If he'd said she needed a change of pace or scenery, then Maria wouldn't have reacted so angrily. He wasn't privy to what Mimi had said to Charity, and he didn't want to know. That was between mother and daughter, and he didn't want to be drawn into the conflict.

"Is she going to live with her brother?"

"No."

"No?" Maria questioned. "Isn't he starting up his own ranch?"

"Yes, Mami. Charity claims living with her brother will not allow her to feel like an adult because Dawson will treat her like she's still his baby sister."

"I understand where she's coming from, because my brothers tried to intimidate every boy who looked at me. They tried it with Jack, but once they discovered he was willing to go toe-to-toe with them they backed off."

Liam smiled. "So, Dad was willing to fight for his woman."

"*Sí.* And that's what you should do if want Charity in your life."

"That's not necessary because she's here in Tenacity and not in Bronco."

"I'm glad she's here," Maria said, smiling, "because I really like her."

"That's makes two of us."

Maria huffed. "Now, when are you going to bring her around again?"

"There's no doubt she's going to be busy trying to find a place then getting settled."

"True. Let her know if she needs things for her kitchen or bathroom, I have a lot of extra stuff packed away she could have."

Liam recalled his mother helping him once he'd moved into his cabin. He'd taken it for granted that all he had to do was move in, but soon realized he'd had to purchase household items. It had taken several years before he'd saved enough money to furnish and decorate the remaining rooms in the two-story house that had become his permanent home.

It was too soon for him to think about sharing his home with Charity. She could no longer live with her parents, and she'd balked about living with her brother, and Liam realized she needed time and space to be on her own. But he'd be there for her, just as he'd promised.

Charity found a vacant one-bedroom on the second floor over a storefront, and she was finally able to exhale after she'd signed the lease. Her mind went into overdrive as she picked up her phone. It had been a week since she'd returned to Tenacity—this time to stay—and whenever she'd exchanged texts with Liam it was to bring him up to date about her apartment search. Now she would have to pay rent, furnish the apartment and stock her refrigerator. It had taken her a while to find a place she could afford, because she wanted to be certain she could manage without her father's wallet, although she hadn't stopped monitoring the Double J's digital footprint

Monitoring her bank balance and budgeting was something she'd never had to do in the past. She lived at home where all her daily needs were met, and her father gave her a generous salary, which she banked, for monitoring the ranch's digital footprint for targeted advertising and protecting the website from cybercriminals and hackers. Charity had caught and eliminated several phishing attacks which could've exposed a lot of the Johns' personal information.

She tapped Liam's number, and he answered after the second ring. Charity smiled when hearing his sonorous greeting.

"Talk to me, beautiful."

"How are you?" she asked.

"That's what I should be asking you."

"I'm good. Great, in fact. Because I finally got an apartment. It's a nice little place over Tiffany Brandt's flower shop."

"Congratulations. When's the housewarming?"

Charity laughed. "That's not going to be for a while because I have to buy furniture before I'm able to move in."

"When do you think that'll be?"

"Hopefully in another week or two. After I hang up with you, I'm going to go online and order something to sleep and sit on. I'm willing to pay for rush delivery because I'm anxious to move in. The apartment could also use a fresh coat of paint, so that's something else on my to-do list."

"Don't worry about painting, bae. I'll help you with that."

"Liam, I don't want—"

"Stop it, Charity," he said in a quiet tone. "You're going to need help, so I'm volunteering to help you."

"Okay. I'll accept your help."

"After I see the apartment, then I'll know how much paint you're going to need."

"Liam?"

"Yes?"

"Thank you."

"You can thank me later once you're settled in, and then we'll have a housewarming."

Charity nodded although he couldn't see her. "I'll be in touch tomorrow."

"I'll be here."

The three words echoed in Charity's head long after the call ended. Liam had promised he would be there for her, and she'd come to believe he would. Even when they didn't see each other, she still felt their connection.

She didn't know how it had happened so quicky. She wasn't falling in love with Liam Martin. She was *in* love with him.

When Charity drove back to the Sanchez house, she immediately sensed something was wrong when she saw

Jameson's vehicle parked in the driveway. She came to a complete stop, shut off the engine, then sat motionless staring through the windshield. When she'd left earlier that morning Dawson hadn't mentioned anything about their brother coming to Tenacity. A number of scenarios tumbled over themselves in her head, and she knew if she didn't go into the house, she would become more agitated with each passing second.

Walking into the house, Charity heard different voices and followed them to the family room where she found all three of her brothers, along with Marisa, Luca and Winter together. "What did I miss?" she asked, smiling. Luca, Dawson, Jameson and Maddox stood up, the four of them staring at her.

Luca reached for his wife's hand, easing her gently to her feet. "We'll see you guys later."

In that instant, Charity realized the Johns had arranged for a family meeting. Her eyes met Marisa's. "Aren't going to follow your brother?"

Marisa shook her head. "No. I'm your sister, so I'm staying."

Charity nodded and smiled. At least she could count on Marisa as an ally in what she predicted would become a united front against her brothers. She sat on the loveseat next to Marisa and gave her brothers a steady stare. "Jameson and Maddox, you must have a damn good reason to drive here from Bronco, and I hope it's not because you miss me. Because I'm not going back." She realized she'd uncovered their subterfuge when they lowered their eyes.

"I asked them to come," Dawson admitted, "because Mom has been blowing up my phone about you telling her that you're never going back to Bronco."

"Come for what, Dawson?" Charity spat out.

"For them to talk some sense into you, because whenever I try to say anything, you just shut me out."

"That's because you don't want to hear whatever it is I want to say."

"And what's that?" Maddox asked.

"To live my life the way I want, not by the rules of someone else who believes they know what's best for me."

"This man you're involved with…" Jameson said.

"What about him?" Charity asked, glaring at the eldest of Randall and Mimi's children.

"Don't you think you're moving too fast with him?"

Charity narrowed her eyes. "Define *fast.*"

"The word is you just met him, and now you're ready to give up your life in Bronco to hook up with him," Jameson explained.

Hook up! Who said anything about hooking up? If I was planning to hook up with Liam, then I would've asked to live with him on the Double M and not waste my time and money looking for an apartment.

"I'm not hooking up with Liam, nor do I plan to hook up with him."

"Maybe he's planning to hook up with you, Charity," Maddox said. "There are a lot of homeless vets with dogs looking for a home, and with you, he found someone willing to give him one."

"Homeless?" Charity and Marisa shouted at the same time.

Dawson frowned. "Who told you Liam Martin was homeless?"

Maddox looked confused. "Our mother said Charity was involved with a poor, homeless veteran."

Dawson pressed a fist to his mouth at the same time he shook his head. "Liam's family owns a successful ranch, the

Double M. They've made their reputation breeding Angus with Santa Gertrudis."

"The Martins settled Montana when it was still a territory," Marisa said, glaring at Maddox. "And for your information, Liam was wounded serving this country and because of his injuries he was given a medical discharge. His dog happens to be highly trained military dog who will risk his life to protect his handler."

Jameson smothered a curse under his breath, while Maddox swallowed a groan. Charity was hard-pressed to conceal a Cheshire cat grin. It served them right for believing everything Mimi told them about Liam and Harley.

Dawson met Charity's eyes. "Even though I like and respect Liam, and I understand you wanting to break free of our parents' iron grip, I think you went about it all wrong."

"That's where you're wrong, Dawson," she countered. "Do you think if I'd decided to live at the Double J that Liam would've been welcomed? You know that answer would be a resounding no. His family are ranchers, but the difference is they're not like the Taylors or Abernathys who own thousands of acres of land and have enough money to establish their own banks." When her brother didn't reply, she continued. "I just signed a lease on an apartment, and tomorrow I will go to the post office to change my address from Bronco to Tenacity."

Dawson rested his head against the back of an armchair. "So, you're really serious about having a relationship with Liam?"

"As serious as you were when you first met Marisa." Her statement was followed by a swollen silence as knowing glances were exchanged between those in the room.

Maddox massaged his forehead with his fingers. "I guess

that settles that. It looks as if our sister has made her mind up about who she wants to be with."

"When are we going to meet our future brother-in-law?" Maddox asked.

Charity felt a rush of heat in her face and chest. "It's too soon to talk about a wedding when Liam and I haven't..." Her words trailed once she realized what she was about to say.

"What are you trying to say, sister?" Jameson teased. "That you and your military boo haven't—"

"That's enough, Jameson," Dawson warned, interrupting him. "There's no need to embarrass our sister. What goes on between her and Liam is not open for discussion."

"Thank you, Dawson," Charity crooned.

He winked at her. "Anytime, sis."

Jameson clasped his hands together. "Now that we've resolved the misunderstanding and learned that Charity's boyfriend isn't a homeless veteran with a dog, I say we go out and get something to eat. My treat."

Charity mouthed a thank-you to Marisa. She knew how she felt about Liam and appreciated her stepping up to support her. She still did not want to believe her brothers had come to Tenacity like a couple of thugs looking to exact revenge on the man taking advantage of their sister. Liam Martin wasn't poor or homeless but a good man with whom she'd fallen in love.

Maddox stood up. "This is your town, Dawson, so what do you suggest?"

"I'm sort of partial to the Grizzly Bar."

Jameson flashed a white-toothed smile. "Then the Grizzly it is."

Dawson looked at Marisa. "You coming?"

She gave Charity a look, who shook her head. "No. I'm going to hang out here with Charity."

"Maybe I'll ask Luca if he wants to join us, because he's probably sleep-deprived and on daddy lockdown."

"Why does my brother have to be on lockdown, Dawson? If he wants to have a boy's night out, then I don't mind babysitting the baby."

Dawson smiled at his wife. "Are you practicing for when we have our little one?"

Charity looked at her brother, then his wife. "Am I missing something?"

"No!" Dawson and Marisa chorused.

But there was something about their denial that told Charity they were hiding something. Were they trying for a baby…or was Marisa already pregnant? And if she was, then a branch of the John family tree would be rooted in Tenacity.

Marisa waited until they were alone to say, "Tell me about your apartment."

"I will. But I want to thank you for having my back."

"That's what sisters are for."

Dawson's wife was right. They'd become sisters in every way and knowing Marisa was there for her would help to make her relocation to Tenacity an easy one.

Charity spent hours on her laptop searching furniture websites, and it was hours past midnight when she finally got into bed. Maddox and Jameson had returned from the Grizzly Bar, claiming they'd eaten and drunk too much while extolling the friendliness of the patrons in the classic western saloon/honkytonk, once Dawson introduced them as his brothers. He'd also convinced them to stay the night rather than attempt to drive back to Bronco.

She teased them saying she wanted to be a fly on the wall once they told Mimi that Liam wasn't homeless but belonged to a family of cattle breeders. Both were disappointed they weren't able to meet the man who was responsible for changing how they now viewed their sister. She was no longer a little girl they had to look after, they'd told her, but a young woman who'd come into her own to control her destiny.

Sleep was elusive as Charity tossed and turned restlessly. She couldn't stop thinking about the audacity of her mother to send her brothers to do her dirty work. She remembered how Liam's parents and siblings had welcomed her with open arms at the Double M when she knew it wouldn't have been the same for Liam if she'd brought him to the Double J.

Charity wasn't certain if Mimi would change her impression of Liam once Maddox and Jameson told her the truth about him, but it wasn't something she wanted to dwell on. And she didn't expect Mimi to apologize for her hurtful words. She just wanted her to respect who she'd chosen to love.

Chapter Thirteen

Liam motioned for Harley to stay, then dropped a kiss onto his mother's cheek. "Don't wait on lunch for me."

He'd planned to pick up paint color chips from the hardware store before meeting Charity at her apartment. She'd sent him a text indicating she'd wanted to get to the apartment early to give it a thorough cleaning before his arrival. Offering to help her paint was what he needed to relieve his restlessness. He still had another two weeks before his father's mandate that he refrain from doing chores ended.

"I'm glad she finally found a place, because when I'd mentioned she was still looking your father suggested she could move into one of the vacant cabins on the ranch in the interim."

"Mami, you forget that Charity has family in Tenacity, so it's not as if she doesn't have a place to lay her head."

"Family she's obviously not willing to continue to live with."

"What are you trying to say, Mami?" Liam had no intention of telling his mother about Charity's confrontation with Mimi. Or how she wanted to be totally emancipated when it came to the Johns.

"Nada."

Liam ran his fingers over his right eyebrow unaware it

had become an unconscious motion. "You can keep telling yourself it's nothing, when we both know what you're up to."

"¿Qué?"

He forced to laugh at his mother's expression. "You feigning innocence is not fooling me."

"You know I like your girlfriend."

"I like her, too, but we don't want to rush into anything. Now that Charity has moved to Tenacity, things will be different between us." Things were different between them because now he was willing to let her into his life.

"How much different?"

Liam groaned. "Enough with the interrogation, Mami." He kissed her again. "I'll see you later."

"No, you won't because I'm not going to put out a plate for you. Treat your girlfriend to a nice dinner to celebrate her move. And don't worry about my grand-dog. I still have several containers of his food in the fridge and a few of those dog biscuits that he likes."

Liam shook his head as he walked out of the house. Maria hadn't tried to be subtle in her attempt to play matchmaker between him and Charity, even resorting to spoiling his dog. Whenever he loaded Harley in the pickup, he would stand up on the rear seats and begin whining once he realized he was going to the main house to see Maria. Even his father had taken to Harley, lying beside the dog on a chaise in the family room to watch movies.

As he headed into town, Liam thought about Maria's suggestion he take Charity out to dinner. It'd been more than a week since he last saw her, and not only had he missed her, he also realized he was crazy in love with her. He'd tried telling himself and rationalizing that he could never have a chance with her because they came from two different worlds. That she had been sheltered and therefore was not worldly enough for him. But he'd seen how their pedigree didn't matter to her and how she'd become a fierce woman and stood up to her mother. While he no longer worried about that, there were still the nightmares. Was he willing to expose her to his PTSD? Would she be willing to stay with him after witnessing one of his nightmares?

Liam stopped at the hardware store and selected paint chips in a wide spectrum of colors ranging from antique white to dark blues before parking along the street behind the rows of stores where Charity had her apartment. He was only a few feet from the door leading to the second-floor apartment over Tiffany in Bloom when he recognized Ellis Corey walking toward the flower shop.

He never had much interaction with the man because Ellis was at least six or seven years his senior, however, Liam was familiar with the Coreys who owned the Circle C. Ellis's sister, Michelle, was a year ahead of him in school.

Smiling, Ellis offered Liam his hand. "Welcome home, soldier."

Liam shook Ellis's hand. "Thanks. Some little birdie told me you threw your Stetson in the ring to run for mayor last year."

Ellis flashed a bright smile. "Yeah. It was all in good fun."

Liam slowly shook his head. "Politics isn't a fun game, Ellis."

"I found that out once I began campaigning. There were a lot of us on the ticket along with a little manipulation and illegal activities, but I'm glad JenniLynn won because she's doing a fine job so far as Tenacity's mayor."

"Enough talk about poli-tricks. My brother Enzo mentioned something about you being engaged to the woman who just happens to own a flower shop here in town."

A smile flittered across the features of the handsome rancher who was never at a loss for female attention. "Guilty as charged."

"Congratulations!"

Ellis nodded. "Thank you. Tiffany's sister is married to Geoff Burris."

Liam whistled softly. "Talk about Black rodeo royalty."

"And speaking of more Black rodeo royalty, my brother Shane is engaged to Remi Hawkins."

"Hot damn!" Liam said through clenched teeth. "Tenacity is about to make folks stand up and be proud of their town now that celebrities are moving here."

"My grandfather keeps saying there's something in the water that when folks come to visit, they decide to stay. The rodeo held during the Dinosaur Days festival was spectacular, and there's talk of hosting one every year in Tenacity like they do in Bronco for the Mistletoe Rodeo."

"I've heard. That's because we love celebrating. It doesn't matter what holiday it's always a party. It's what I missed most, aside from my family, when I was away."

"Now that you are back don't be a stranger. You know we Coreys host a Fall Frolic every October, so I expect you to attend along with the rest of the Martins."

Liam smiled. "I wouldn't miss it." He waited for Ellis to enter the flower shop before he opened the storefront door leading to Charity's apartment. He climbed the staircase, stopping on the landing and ringing the doorbell.

"Who is it?"

"It's the big bad wolf ready to blow your house down."

Charity opened the door, flashing her trademark bright smile. "You would if my house was made of straw."

Liam couldn't take his eyes off her as she opened the door wider. She'd covered her hair with a bandana, and it was hard to discern the shape of her figure under an oversized T-shirt and baggy cotton pants. She'd exchanged her expensive footwear for a pair of well-worn running shoes.

He shouldered the door close and reached for her. "You look as if you've been working very hard."

Holding her close, inhaling the faint scent of perfume clinging to her moist body and staring into the trusting eyes that had snared him in a web of longing from which he did not want to escape, Liam knew for certain she was the woman he wanted in his life.

Lowering his head, he kissed her. Gently as if he feared she would break, then deepened the kiss until her lips parted under his. The passion he'd kept in check flared like an uncontrolled fire. He tightened his hold around her body and lifted her off her feet. Liam sought to devour her mouth when it was her entire body he'd wanted to taste.

Charity wound her arms around Liam's neck, clinging to him as if he was a lifeline that would keep her from drowning in an ocean of wanting. She'd never experienced a feeling like this before. She loved his patience, gentleness and his respect for her as her own person. And more importantly he hadn't attempted to change who she was.

Even when she tried to rationalize that moving from Bronco to Tenacity was nothing more than an act of rebellion, Charity realized it was only a half-truth. She'd fallen in love and grown up at the same time, and she had Liam to thank for both.

"Charity?" Her name came out like a groan.

"Yes, Liam?"

"I love you."

If he hadn't been holding her, Charity knew she would fallen because her heart was beating so fast that she felt lightheaded. He loved her and she loved him. "And I love you so much that my heart feels as if it's going to explode from the joy you bring me," she whispered.

Liam lowered her feet to the floor. "I don't want to talk about paint colors now."

She met his large brown eyes. "What do you want to talk about?"

"Us."

"What about us, Liam?"

"Where do we go from here?"

Charity was becoming confused. They'd admitted to being in love with each other, so what else was there to discuss? She'd moved to Tenacity, and they would pick up where they'd left off before the Bronco military fundraiser.

"I don't understand," she said.

"I need to know if you're all-in when it comes to us. That if something happens you won't go running back to Bronco, because there are times when I'm in a dark place."

Now she was totally confused. "You're talking in riddles, Liam. I told you I love you, and that means I'm with you for the long haul and that means if or whenever you're in that dark place. Couples have their ups and downs, and because we're individuals we're not going to agree on everything, but that doesn't mean I'm going to throw a hissy fit and walk away from you when you need me most. And hopefully you won't walk away from me."

Liam shook his head. "That's never going to happen." He stared at something over her head. "Will you come home with me?"

Charity stared at him as the seconds ticked. "To the Double M?"

A hint of a smile lifted the corners of Liam's mouth. "That is home for me."

"But…but I look a mess." *Girl, why are you acting stupid when the man is inviting you to his house? He knows what you look like.*

"You look beautiful. Come with me. Please."

"I'm coming. I just have to get my tote."

Charity didn't remember locking the apartment door or getting into Liam's vehicle until she sat beside him as he drove to the Double M. What she didn't want was for his parents, his mother in particular, to see her looking unkempt and bedraggled. She'd gotten up earlier that morning and gathered enough cleaning supplies to sweep and mop floors, give the bathroom a thorough cleaning and even wash windows. She'd only stopped long enough to drink a travel mug of coffee, but nothing else.

Taking off the bandana, she removed the elastic band holding her hair in place, tangled strands falling down around her face and shoulders. Why had she let Liam talk her into going to his home looking like something the cat drug in?

He took her hand and brought it to his lips for a quick kiss. "Stop playing with your hair, Charity. I told you before that you look beautiful."

She groaned. "My hair looks like a mop. I'm not wearing any makeup, and my clothes are frumpy. If you think I look beautiful, you may need to have your eyes checked."

Liam gave her a quick glance. "There's nothing wrong with my vision. We're going to my home, not the Association."

Charity pulled her hand back. Was he comparing his home to the private club because he continued to believe they were from different worlds? She'd given up the lifestyle to which she'd been born to move to Tenacity, and yet it sounded as if he was holding on to the theory of them being so different.

"What are you implying, Liam?"

"Do you really think I care if you wear makeup? It's not about the outward appearance but what inside that makes me love you, Charity. You moved to Tenacity so you can be yourself, and if you feel comfortable going out in public without makeup, then embrace it. No one is going to judge you. After you've lived here a while you'll notice that even the well-to-do folks who move from Bronco learn to fit in rather than stand out. Tenacity has gone through some rough times, yet we're still standing. We've had our share of scandals like most places, but we move on from there. Luca discovering some dinosaur bones has breathed new life in the town, and even though Marco claims there are rumors that no new bones have been found, Tenacity still hums with an undercurrent of excitement because folks are optimistic and most of all we're survivors."

Charity stared out at the passing landscape. She didn't know why but suddenly she felt like child who was being chastised for something she'd shouldn't have done. She'd endured enough of that from her parents and she didn't want to continue it with Liam. She'd become so used to taking offense whenever her parents said something to which she didn't agree that she was ready for a verbal confrontation. And now it was the same thing with Liam whenever she'd become defensive. He'd talked not wanting to engage in verbal confrontation, meanwhile she'd reverted to a shrew whenever he said something she'd felt the need to defend.

Her mood changed when she noticed him drive past the main house and head in the direction of his cabin. He pulled around to the rear and parked.

"Honey, I'm home," he said in a spot-on Ricky Ricardo imitation of Desi Arnaz calling to Lucille Ball.

Charity was out of the pickup before he could come around to assist her. Reaching for her tote, she smiled up at him when he took her free hand. "Should I take my shoes off?" She recalled him mentioning that Maria had such a policy at her home.

"Nah. You're good. It's the boots we wear when working on the ranch that we take off. I don't have time to differentiate between work and regular ones."

She waited while he removed his boots, set them on a rack, then slipped on a pair of running shoes he should've discard long ago. "Those have seen better days."

"True. I should ask you to help me go through my closet now that I'm back to weed out what I don't wear or doesn't fit so they can be donated to the church's outreach." He pointed to his shoes. "These, however, will not be included." He flashed her a grin.

"They should be the first item on your list, Liam." Charity followed him through the mudroom and into an all-white and stainless-steel kitchen. "I love your kitchen."

He bowed his head as if she were royalty. "Thank you. It's my favorite room in the house. The dining room is second. However, I rarely eat there. The exception is when I have company."

"Am I considered company?"

"Nope. You're practically family."

She smiled. "Lucky me."

"No, Charity. I'm the one with the luck to have someone like you in my life. You're like a ray of sunshine."

Smiling, Charity sang the lyrics to Stevie Wonder's hit "You Are the Sunshine of My Life."

* * *

Liam stared at the woman with whom he'd fallen in love, listening to her perfect pitch as she launched into a rendition of the classic tune. Charity truly had a gifted voice. He applauded once she finished, she appearing somewhat embarrassed by his response.

"How often do you put on personal one-on-one concerts?" he teased.

"Never."

"Now that I'm been thoroughly entertained, what's your preference? Breakfast or brunch? Don't look so shocked, princess. I heard your stomach making noises when I kissed you. When was the last time you ate?"

Charity lowered her eyes. "I had dinner last night, but only coffee this morning, because I wanted to get to the apartment early enough to begin cleaning before you got there."

"That could've waited, Charity."

"No, it couldn't. I'm expecting a delivery of the bedroom furniture the day after tomorrow."

"If that's the case, then we'll begin painting the bedroom this afternoon. Meanwhile, you need to eat. Breakfast or brunch?" he repeated.

"Brunch."

"What would you like?"

"An omelet."

"What kind of omelet?"

"Oh, I have a choice?" Charity asked.

"With me you'll always have a choice, Charity. If we're going to be together, then it can't me my way or no way, or vice versa."

She smiled. "Okay. I'd like to order a Western omelet.

Meanwhile, would you mind if I took a tour of your house until brunch is ready?"

"Not at all. *Mi casa es tu casa.*"

"I understood that."

"What about *eres lo major que me ha passado*?" Liam questioned.

"What does that mean?"

Liam winked at her. "You'll find out soon enough."

Charity was offered a glimpse into what her life would be like after spending time touring Liam's home and sharing brunch. His house was spotless which meant he was a neat-freak. And if they hadn't made plans to go the hardware store to select paint colors, she would've been content to fall asleep on a chaise in the enclosed back porch.

At Strom and Son, Liam purchased a ladder, rollers, brushes, painter's tape, drop cloths and the paint she'd chosen—teal paint for the bedroom, a soft peachy shade for the living room/dining area and antique white for the miniscule bathroom. He'd exchanged his jeans and shirt for old faded ones and his boots for a grungy-looking pair. All the paint contained primer, which would save a lot of time by not having to go over the walls twice.

They made quick work of painting the bedroom before shifting their attention to the living room, and that was when she noticed he was having difficulty climbing up and down the ladder, which probably was a result of his injuries.

Charity took the brush from him, and not wanting to injure his pride, she said, "I'll finish the rest of the ceiling. You've done enough for one day."

"Are you sure?"

She smiled. "Of course I'm sure, Liam. This happens to not be my first rodeo. One year I decided I was tired of looking at the bland white walls in my bedroom, so I painted them a bright iridescent pink. Talk about hard on the eyes."

Liam sat on the floor and extended his legs. "How long did you live with the color?"

"Less than a week. It took two coats of primer to cover the pink before I repainted the room in a calming oyster white."

He smiled. "That will learn you."

"It sure did." She looked around the living room. "After I finish the ceiling, I believe we're done."

"You did good, princess."

"*We* did good. If you hadn't helped me, it would've taken me at least three days to paint the entire apartment."

"What's next?" Liam asked.

"Making it look lived-in. I bought several colorful scatter rugs, floor cushions that will double as chairs from Nothin' New. I'm seriously thinking about buying a wooden crate I saw there and turning it into a coffee table."

"Was that your first time buying things from a consignment shop?" Liam asked Charity.

She climbed down off the ladder and gave him a direct stare. "Yes. Why?"

"Because I feel bad that you were forced to choose me over your family and give up the financial security many people would kill for."

"Money doesn't matter to me, Liam."

"Of course, it doesn't because you never had to do without it or you wouldn't say something like that."

Charity felt hurt by his comment yet knew he was right. Not having money to buy whatever she wanted had never been an issue. The John name alone opened doors few would ever conceive of entering.

It was becoming more and more difficult for her to figure out the man who'd confessed to loving her. When he'd invited her to his home, she initially thought he'd wanted to make love, not feed her. It wasn't that she didn't appreciate his concern for her well-being, but she wondered what there was about her that wouldn't allow him to let her in fully. He had to know by her response to his kiss she'd wanted more, and the more was their making love.

Liam pushed to his feet. "I'll walk you to your car, then I'm going to head home."

She managed a tired smile. He was going home, while she was going back to the Sanchezes for a warm bath, followed by a glass of wine, then nighty-night.

After she locked up, Liam reached for her hand and they walked to her car.

"What's on your schedule for tomorrow?" he asked her.

"I'm planning to sleep in late, then do some shopping. I need to buy things for my kitchen and bathroom."

"Send me a list of what you need, because my mother has stuff with tags on them still. Towels, pots and pans. She won't admit it, but she can't resist buying things for the house."

"She wouldn't mind giving me some?"

"Not at all. When I told her you were setting up an apartment she offered."

"Your mother is truly one of a kind." *And so is mine. But in a different way.* Charity hadn't spoken to her mother since she'd moved to Tenacity, and that was the way she preferred it. If Mimi couldn't treat her like an adult, then it was better for them not to speak.

"Now you sound like my dad. He worships the ground his wife walks on."

Charity nodded. "I saw that when I came to your fish

fry. Even though I was sitting between your parents I noticed he kept staring at her."

"Even after thirty-five years of marriage they still act like teenagers. They couldn't wait for us to move out of the main house so they could have it all to themselves. There were times when we teased them about giving us another brother or even a sister, and that was when Dad went into military-mode to shut us down."

Charity knew if she were ever to have children, she would rear them differently from how Randall and Mimi raised their offspring. There would be none of the rules about who they could or could not marry.

Liam walked her to where she'd parked, brushed a light kiss on her mouth, then waited while she got into her vehicle and drove away. In a few days, once most her furniture was delivered, she would move into her new place to begin her new life in Tenacity.

Chapter Fourteen

Liam walked into Tiffany's flower shop to look for a plant for Charity's apartment. She had invited him over for dinner and a private housewarming. It only had taken days for her to make her little place appear as if she'd lived there for a while. She'd put up framed prints on the walls, covered portions of the floor with colorful scatter rugs and covered the top of a wooden crate with rattan placemats. She'd spared no expense when purchasing a computer desk/table and chair, and he wondered if her father had continued to pay her to monitor the Double J's digital footprint or if he'd cut her off financially. He knew whenever he mentioned money to Charity it was if a wall would go up between them, so he promised himself not to broach the subject.

"Hello again," Tiffany said, greeting him with a warm smile and a wave. The diamond ring on her left hand symbolized her engagement to Ellis Corey. "Are you looking for another bouquet of flowers?"

"No," he laughed. "This time I'd like a plant. It's a housewarming gift."

"Hanging, ferns, flowering or succulents?"

Here we go again. Why is she making me choose? "Let me look around, and I'll let you know." There were so many different varieties of plants that Liam felt slightly overwhelmed. He didn't know if Charity had a green thumb or what plant was easy to care for.

"What do you suggest?" he asked Tiffany.

"If you're not certain what the person would like, then I suggest succulents. They're hardy and don't require much watering."

"Okay. I'll take the succulents." He watched Tiffany select a rectangular glazed pot with hand-painted Asian symbols. "Nice." He waited for Tiffany to wrap the pot in clear cellophane, tie it with a jade-green ribbon, then place it in a shopping bag stamped with the shop's logo.

"I hope she'll like it."

Liam tapped his credit card. "I'm certain she will."

Humming to himself he went up the staircase and rapped lightly on the door. It opened in seconds, and he was met with music and mouthwatering aromas. Liam leaned over and kissed Charity, inhaling the hypnotic scent of her perfume.

"You look and smell incredible."

Her hair was a mass of tiny golden curls. She hadn't worn any makeup, and with her bare face she appeared so natural and refreshing. A light blue flower-sprigged sundress displayed a lot more skin than he was used to seeing on her. How, he wondered, was he going to make it through the dinner and not make love to her? It was becoming harder and harder for Liam to restrain himself when he was with Charity when all he thought about was seducing her. And there were just so many cold showers he could take! All she had to do was give him a sign, say one word and they would end up in bed together. He'd told himself that he was trying to be a gentleman because he didn't want Charity to think she was making a mistake giving up all she had for him. He wanted to be worthy of what she'd sacrificed to be with him.

"Thank you." She stared at the colorful shopping bag. "What did you bring?"

"Something for your housewarming."

Charity took the bag, peering inside. "Oh, my goodness. How did you know that I like succulents?"

"I didn't. Tiffany helped me select the plant. She did the same when I sent you the bouquet of flowers."

"She must have second sight, because I loved the flowers and I love this plant. I'm going to put it on the window ledge in the front to catch the sunlight."

Liam unbuttoned his cuffs and rolled back the sleeves on a chambray shirt. "Can I help you with anything?"

"You can carve the chicken. I just took it out of the oven to let it rest. The garlic mashed potatoes and green beans are also done." She held up a glass. "But first, white wine or rosé?"

"It doesn't matter," he said as he made his way to the bathroom to wash his hands. He wanted to tell Charity he didn't need or want wine. He wanted *her*.

Forty minutes later, sitting on a pillow opposite Charity, Liam touched the corners of his mouth with a napkin. The makeshift coffee table was crowded with the remains of their dinner. He picked up his wineglass and held it toward her. "To the cook. And or the best that's yet to come," he said, meeting her eyes.

Charity nodded. "To love."

He took a sip of the still chilled rosé, held it in his mouth before letting it slowly slide down his throat. The wine was excellent and the woman smiling at him was exquisite, and he wondered how he got so lucky. And it wasn't for the first time that he'd reminded himself that he had survived when Dean Valentini hadn't, because he was fated to meet a woman Dean had briefly dated. He thought about what his father had said about meeting the woman who would make his world and everything in it as close to perfect as it could be. And Liam knew for certain that Charity John was that woman. With her he would be able to face his demons where they would eventually no longer become a part of his life and their future.

Music from Charity's phone's playlist flowing from an external speaker provided the backdrop for a night filled with delicious food and sparkling conversation, and Liam knew it was an encounter he wanted to repeat again and again. He'd never felt more content to sit on the pillows, drink wine and laugh, about everything from the childhood pranks he'd played on his brothers to the crazy antics of reality TV.

"Do you think people actually believe these shows?" he asked her.

"Of course, Liam. Otherwise, they wouldn't be renewed year after year."

"Do you believe them?"

She peered at him over the rim of her glass. "Not all of them. Some of the episodes are so over the top."

"That's because parts of the shows are scripted. Flipping tables and throwing drinks make for dramatic programing."

"Oh, so you know about flipping tables?" Charity teased.

"I've seen a few when dudes have had too much to drink."

"So, it's not only women who flip tables."

"There are soldiers who should've stopped at a couple of drinks but then get into a fight and literally wreck a place."

"What happens to them?"

"They end up court-martialed."

"Have you ever been in a bar fight?"

Liam shook his head. "Never. A couple of glasses of beer or wine is my limit. I've never been able to tolerate hard liquor."

"Good for you."

"What's good for me is meeting you," he countered, giving her a long, penetrating stare.

"Liam," she whispered.

"That's my name, sweetheart."

Liam wondered if at that moment Charity was experiencing what he was feeling. That the sexual tension between them was so strong it was palpable. That they'd escaped into their own cocoon of longing that had to be resolved or they would combust. She whispered his name again, the sound pregnant with longing, and he knew the kiss he gave her was going to lead somewhere different from when they'd kissed at the picnic. He wanted her and she wanted him, and this time he was prepared.

He stood up, extending his hand and pulling her effortlessly to her feet. Liam swept Charity up into his arms and carried her into the bedroom. The blinds were partially drawn, allowing for ribbons of light across the bed.

No words were spoken; there was just the sound of measured breathing as he reached into the pocket of his jeans and placed a condom on the bedside table. Charity smiled, her eyes never straying from his. Liam took off his clothes, watching for her reaction to his bared chest and biceps peppered with scars he'd sustained in the blast. There were expanses of skin that had been grafted in order to match that on his face. A small cry escaped her parted lips at the same time her eyes filled with tears.

"It's okay," he whispered. *Sweet heaven, please don't let her start crying.* He didn't want or need her pity.

Charity sat up and slipped the thin straps of her dress off her shoulders. In a motion so perfect it could have been choreographed they undressed themselves until they were completely naked. She extended a hand to him. "I need you."

She needed him, and Liam needed her. He needed Charity to help erase the horrors he relived over and over once he'd emerged from the medically-induced coma. Dreams that haunted him relentlessly and not permitting him a restful night's sleep. In that instant Liam realized Charity was the woman in his latest nightmare. She was the image of a young woman with blond hair and blue eyes who'd reached out to pull him to safety.

Liam got into bed with Charity, supporting his greater weight on his forearms as he cradled her face and took possession of her mouth. Everything in his lovemaking was slow, because he wanted to take his time tasting and savoring all of her. He'd become a sculptor, his mouth charting a path from her lips and down her body, lingering between her thighs to her feet before reversing and turning her over to taste every inch of flesh beginning with the curve of her rounded buttocks to the nape of her neck. He registered the change in her breathing when he found an erogenous zone, and whenever she moaned, he'd lingered there.

Charity was floating out of her body. Then she felt as if she was drowning, pulled by an undertow of erotic sensations that heated the blood coursing through her veins. Never had she experienced lovemaking that threatened to hurl her beyond the point of no return. Electricity seemed to arc through her when she felt the beginnings of an orgasm.

"Please, please," she repeated shamelessly. "I need to

feel you inside me." Her pleas faded when Liam paused to slip on protection. He joined their bodies, and together they found a rhythm where they ceased to exist as separate entities and became one with the other. She'd barely returned from her free-fall flight when Liam groaned and then breathed out the last of his passion into her mouth. They lay together, limbs entwined, waiting until their breathing slowed to a normal rhythm. She emitted a small protest when he pulled out and left the bed to discard the condom. He returned, and within minutes she'd fallen asleep, sheltered in his arms.

Charity wasn't certain how long she'd been sleeping when she woke to find Liam moaning as if in pain. Rising on an elbow, she watched as he continued moaning, mumbling words she couldn't make out, then screaming and thrashing about while in the throes of a terrifying nightmare. Then without warning, he opened his eyes and what she saw frightened her. They were wild, filled with fear.

"Liam, are you okay?" She reached out to him, but he sat up and got out bed, reaching for his clothes. She stared at the tattoo of a large dog on his left forearm. "Please talk to me."

"Leave me alone."

Charity registered the coldness in his voice. "Please tell me what's the matter."

Liam continued to put his clothes on, unable and unwilling to share the horror and ugliness of what he'd endured over the past six months. There were the screams, the blood, the moans and the prayers of those hoping to die. The images and sounds were stamped on his brain like the permanent tattoo on his arm. No, he reasoned. A tattoo that could be removed by a laser. The images and sounds would be with him forever.

Charity rose to her knees, then sat on the heels of her feet. "Talk to me."

He glared at her. "No!"

"Why not?"

"Why not, Charity? Because you don't know me as well as you think. Maybe we made a mistake becoming involved so quickly. And you probably would've been better off staying in Bronco rather than moving here. Go back to your mother and tell her you're sorry. That she was right about you not getting involved with me."

Liam turned his back when the tears in her eyes spilled onto her cheeks. He didn't want to hurt her, but having her witness him reliving his nightmares was something he hadn't wanted to put her through. He loved her too much for that.

He left the apartment, knowing he'd lied to Marisa. He'd promised her he would never walk away from Charity. And that's exactly what he was doing. He was walking away to save her from having to deal with a man who was as emotionally damaged as he was physically.

"Why do you look as if you've lost your best friend?" Marisa asked Charity.

She'd invited Marisa to her apartment to show her how she'd decorated it. Her sister-in-law was her second visitor and the first since Liam had walked out two days ago. "It's because I did," she confirmed. She told her sister-in-law about witnessing Liam having a nightmare that initially frightened her, then broke her heart as she realized he was experiencing PTSD. "It wasn't until he'd taken off his shirt that I saw where he'd been wounded. I kept asking him to talk to me, but he refused."

"Maybe he's not ready to share that part of his life with you, Charity."

"Why not? And when is he going to be ready? He told me that he loved me, so why can't he trust me enough to talk about what happened to him when he was overseas?"

"Liam is a good man, and if you hope to have a future with him, then you're going to have to give him time and space to open up to you."

"The difference is I changed my life, Marisa. He could at least meet me halfway. He's admitted to having PTSD, and there are times when he was in a dark place, and I've accepted that, so why can't he open up to me about what happened to him?"

"Have you thought that maybe he's not able to change for you? That what he went through he may never reveal to anyone? Remember, you're the woman he loves, not his psychiatrist."

"Are you saying I should stay in my lane?"

Marisa huffed. "No, Charity. I'm trying to tell you that you can't force Liam to open up to you if that's something he's unwilling to do. He hasn't been back in Tenacity a month, and he has to get used to being a civilian after eight years as a soldier. You told me a man you'd dated died in the same explosion that almost cost Liam his life, so that has to be traumatic for him. And more importantly, you have to be someone very special for him to admit that he loves you."

"I love him, Marisa."

"And love isn't turned on and off like a faucet. If you and Liam are meant to be together, it will happen."

"I hope you're right."

"I know I'm right," Marisa said. "I don't want to change

the subject, but have you heard that no more dinosaur bones were found at the digging site?"

Charity nodded. She recalled Liam mentioning that his brother had overheard the same news. "What's going to happen now?"

"Everyone was hoping it would be the cure-all for some of Tenacity's ailments, but the only good news is that the Bruckner brothers are talking about leaving town."

"Good riddance to those hustlers," Charity spat out.

"Word," drawled Marisa. "What we need is another fundraising event like we had in April for Dinosaur Days." She paused. "Wait a minute. Weren't you a part of a fundraising committee in Bronco a couple of weeks ago?"

"Yes! Bronco hosts Presents for Patriots every year to support their military veterans. That's something we can do here, because Liam can't be the only veteran who is grappling with issues tied to his military service. People tend to be very generous around the holidays, but former soldiers need support all year long."

"Liam's father is also ex-military. I think you're onto something, Charity. We can put our heads together and come up with ideas for a concert."

"And putting on a concert should be easy for you given the success of Bronco's Mistletoe Pageant. How soon do you think we can pull this off?"

Marisa pressed her palms together as if she were praying. "We have to ask the mayor for her approval. And once we get it, we should be able to finalize everything before the end of the month."

Charity scrunched up her nose. "That's less than ten days."

"We'll use social media to get the word out, and we can

print up flyers for merchants to hand out to their customers."

"What about talent?" Charity asked.

"That's easy. I know enough folks in Tenacity who would love performing before a live crowd. Besides, there are a few aspiring musicians who hang out at the Social Club that I can ask if they're willing to sign up. Of course, your name will be on the list of performers."

"Yeah right. I'll be among those who sing about having loved and lost."

"Stop it, Charity. You haven't lost Liam."

"He told me I should go back to Bronco."

"Well, it's apparent you didn't take his advice because you're still here. And he probably said it not to hurt you but to put some distance between the two of you until he can get his head together."

"What he doesn't know is that I'm not going back. I'm enjoying my newfound independence. Once we finalize the plans for the fundraiser, I'll text to let him know about it. Maybe he will or maybe he won't attend, and at this point I don't much care, because I can't see myself chasing after a man who doesn't want to be with me."

"I'm going to contact JenniLynn and ask her if we can use the auditorium in the Town Hall, that's if she and the town council will approve the event."

"Jack, you need to talk to your son. Whenever I talk to him, all I get is either a grunt or a one-syllable answer."

Jack Martin didn't glance up from the newspaper spread out on the table in front of him. "Babe, you need to lighten up on the boy. He's been through a lot."

Maria glared at her husband. "Liam's not a boy but a twenty-six-year-old man."

Jack's head popped. "Who's dealing with a lot of shit, Maria." He ignored his wife's gasp; he rarely used profanity in her presence. "Yeah, I said it. He's suffering from PTSD and he's struggling to hide it. But I've seen enough soldiers who've dealt with it to know what Liam is going through."

"You didn't tell me he had PTSD."

"That's because he made me promise not to say anything to you."

"But I'm his mother."

"And because you are he didn't want to upset you. Like you are now."

Maria sat down heavily in a kitchen chair. "Oh, my poor baby."

"Oh, now he's your baby?" Jack taunted.

"Jack Martin, you know right well what I'm talking about."

He nodded and smiled. "Of course I do. I believe there's something else that's also bothering him."

"What?"

"Not a what but a who. I think he broke up with his girlfriend."

"Charity?" Maria asked. "I was under the assumption that they were getting pretty serious about each other."

"So, did I. Maybe they just hit rough patch."

Maria held her forehead. "It probably more like a speed bump if she moved here to be with him."

"I have a lot faith in my sons. They'll get their love lives together one of these days, and you'll get the grandchildren you want instead of lavishing all of your attention on your so-called grand-dog."

Maria hoped it would happen for Liam because she knew

Charity John was good for him and he for her. And there was no doubt she loved her son if she was willing to move to Tenacity to be with him.

Chapter Fifteen

Liam was shocked when he received a text from Charity that she was participating in a concert and hoped he would attend. He'd heard her sing and was curious to see how she would perform in front of a live audience.

Since the night he'd walked away from her Liam found himself engaging in monologues with Harley about being a fool for shutting Charity out of his life because he was afraid to let her in and see the emotional toll of the explosion he had to endure.

He'd lost track of the number of times he'd picked up the phone to call her, only to set it aside. Liam knew he'd said things that hurt her but he didn't know how to prove to her he was sorry. He would attend the concert to support her. It was the least he could do to support the woman he loved.

The day of the scheduled concert Liam took Harley with him when he drove into town and stopped at Tiffany's shop to buy flowers for Charity to present to her after the concert. Even though they were no longer dating he still loved her and wanted to support her performance. He glanced up at the window of her apartment to find the potted succulent. She'd kept his housewarming gift.

Tiffany greeted him with a warm smile when he walked in. "Hello, stranger. I haven't seen you around lately."

"I been staying close to the ranch. I'd like to pick up a bouquet."

"Charity is one lucky woman, because it isn't often that I get repeat customers for couples who are still together."

"Charity and I are just friends."

"Yeah right. Like Ellis and I are just friends."

Liam wasn't about to try and convince Tiffany that he and Charity weren't still together, because he didn't have it in him. "I'd like the same flowers you selected for me when I first came in."

"That's peonies, lilacs and freesias."

He smiled. "You remembered."

"I make it my business to remember what all my customers like."

Tiffany created a bouquet that was even more gorgeous than the first one he'd ordered. Liam thanked her, then followed the crowd rushing toward the town hall to get there before the concert began.

He found a seat in the back of the auditorium, at the end of the aisle, and Harley sat on his left. He waited patiently for Charity to take the stage. Liam had to admit there was a lot of musical talent in his hometown. Some of the performers had musicians accompany them, while most had prerecorded tracks. He suddenly sat forward on his seat when Charity appeared on stage, the spotlight bathing her in gold. Liam closed his eyes, his chest tightening when he recognized the familiar piano opening to "I Can't Make You Love Me."

He covered his face with one hand and struggled to breathe, but the band of tightness across his chest wouldn't allow him to exhale without experiencing discomfort. It finally released him, and he opened his eyes to watch her pour out her heart in a song. Liam heard the pleading in her voice. It was the same tone he recalled when she'd pleaded with him to talk to her. He did love her. More than any other woman he'd ever known.

He'd acted like a fool and pushed her away, shut her out of his life when he should have let her in. Liam was still frozen in in his seat when Charity was joined on stage by Marisa and JenniLynn Garrett. The mayor thanked musical director Marisa Sanchez-John, who was responsible for the musical talent, and Charity John for her work in putting together the concert to raise funds to support veterans in Tenacity.

It was the second time that month he'd witnessed Charity's involvement in a plan to support military veterans, and he knew she'd done it for him. She hadn't been able to help him directly, but she had come up with something to support him indirectly.

He waited until after the show to approach her. She appeared genuinely surprised to see him. "Harley and I would like to give you something." He handed the bouquet to the dog, and Charity bent down to take it.

"Thank you, Harley." She looked up at Liam. "And thank you, Liam. They're beautiful."

"I don't know how to tell you how sorry I am for what I said to you. I'm no different from your parents in not respecting you as an adult."

Charity shook her head. "There's no need to apologize, Liam."

"Yes, there is, because I love you. I believe I fell in love with you the first time I saw you because something beyond our control connected us. And when you love someone, you have to trust them. I was wrong thinking you needed to be protected from my suffering from PTSD, and I didn't want what happened to me to affect your life where you'd fear being with me."

Charity took a step, bringing them less than a foot apart. "Whatever you'd gone through, that's a part of you. But whatever you will go through that will be a part of us. I love you, Liam, and I promise never to abandon you no matter what happens between us."

"What do you want to happen, Charity?"

"It's all up to you. Remember, you walked away from me."

"And that was the biggest mistake I've ever made in my life."

"This concert is the beginning of a military support organization called Tenacity Turns Up. I'm planning to use the money I saved after graduating college, my salary for managing the online presence of the Double J and some funds from a number of strategic investments as a start-up for the organization. I'm prepared to do this whether or not you and I will be together."

"I believe you're going to need a partner who knows the ins and out of the military."

"Oh, really?"

Liam winked at her. "Yes, really."

"Who do you have in mind?"

"You're looking at him."

Charity crossed her arms under her breasts. "I think I'm going to need some convincing that you're best man for the position."

"What do I have to do?"

"Take me to the Double M so we can talk about it."

"May I make suggestion?"

"Of course."

"I think we have to do a lot of talking that may take place over, say, several days or maybe even a week. What say you pack a bag with enough clothes to last you for the duration?"

Charity gave him a smile that he couldn't resist. "That sounds like a plan."

Liam leaned in and kissed her, not caring who was looking. He'd been given a second chance, and this time he intended to make it work.

* * * * *